DARK SIDE OF THE STREET

Jack Higgins

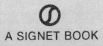

A SIGNET BOOK

PUBLISHER'S NOTE

This is a work of fiction. Names, characters, places, and incidents either are the product of the author's imagination or are used fictitiously, and any resemblance to actual persons, living or dead, events, or locales is entirely coincidental.

NAL BOOKS ARE AVAILABLE AT QUANTITY DISCOUNTS WHEN USED TO PROMOTE PRODUCTS OR SERVICES. FOR INFORMATION PLEASE WRITE TO PREMIUM MARKETING DIVISION, NEW AMERICAN LIBRARY, 1633 BROADWAY, NEW YORK, NEW YORK 10019.

Copyright © 1967 by Martin Fallon

SIGNET TRADEMARK REG. U.S. PAT. OFF. AND FOREIGN COUNTRIES
REGISTERED TRADEMARK—MARCA REGISTRADA
HECHO EN DRESDEN, TN, U.S.A.

SIGNET, SIGNET CLASSIC, MENTOR, ONYX, PLUME, MERIDIAN and NAL BOOKS are published by New American Library, a division of Penguin Books USA Inc., 1633 Broadway, New York, New York 10019

First Signet Printing, May, 1984

5 6 7 8 9 10 11 12 13

PRINTED IN THE UNITED STATES OF AMERICA

1

War Game

Somewhere across the moor gunfire rumbled menacingly, strangely subdued in the heat of the afternoon, and below in the quarry where the prisoners laboured stripped to the waist there was a sudden stir of interest.

Ben Hoffa worked in the shadow of the north face amongst a jumble of great blocks of slate and he paused as he swung the ten pound hammer above his head and lowered it slowly to look up towards the distant hills, a hand shading his eyes from the sun.

He was a small man in his late thirties, muscular and wiry with good shoulders, his hair prematurely grey, the eyes as cold and hard as the blocks of slate around him. His partner, O'Brien, a tall, stolid Irishman, loosened the crowbar he was holding with easy strength and straightened, a frown on his face.

"And what in the hell would that be?"

"Field Artillery," Hoffa told him.

O'Brien stared at him blankly. "You must be joking."

"Summer manœuvres—the Army hold them every year around this time.

In the distance, three transport planes moved over the horizon and as they watched, a line of silken canopies fluttered open as men stepped into space to float down like thistledown blown on a summer breeze. The sensation of space and complete freedom was so acute that O'Brien was conscious of a sudden aching emptiness in his stomach. His hands gripped the crowbar convulsively and Hoffa shook his head.

"Not a chance, Paddy, you wouldn't get five miles."

O'Brien dropped the crowbar to the ground and wiped the sweat from his forehead with the back of a hand. "It makes you think, though."

"The first five years are the worst," Hoffa said, his face expressionless.

There was the crunch of a boot on loose stones behind them, O'Brien glanced over his shoulder and reached for the crowbar. "Parker," he said simply.

Hoffa showed no particular interest and continued to watch the paratroopers drift down behind the breast of the moor three of four miles away as the young prison officer approached. In spite of the heat, there was a touch of guardsman-like elegance about the neatly starched open-neck shirt with its military-style epaulettes and the tilt of the uniform cap over the eyes.

He paused a yard or two away, the staff in his right hand moving menacingly. "And what in the hell do you think you're on, Hoffa?" he demanded harshly. "A Sunday School outing?"

Hoffa turned, glanced at him casually and without speaking, spat on his palms, swung the hammer high and brought it down squarely on the head of the crowbar, splitting the block of slate in two with an insolent grace.

"All right, Paddy," he said to the Irishman, "let's have another."

For all the notice he had taken of him, Parker might not have existed. For a moment, the prison officer stood there, his face white and then he turned suddenly and walked away.

"You want to watch it, Ben," O'Brien said. "He'll have you, that one. If it takes all year, he'll have you."

"That's what I'm counting on," Hoffa said and ignoring the expression of shocked amazement that appeared on the Irishman's face, he swung the hammer high above his head and brought it down again with unerring aim.

Hagen, the Principal Officer, stood by one of the Land-Rovers at the top of the dirt road that led into the quarry and smoked a cigarette, a black and tan Alsatian crouched at his feet. He was a tall heavily built man nearing retirement and a thirty year sentence spent at various of Her Majesty's Prisons had failed to erase an expression of natural kindliness from the pleasant bronzed face.

He watched Parker approach, aware from the set of the man's shoulders that something was wrong and sighed heavily. Amazing how difficult some people made it for themselves.

"What's wrong now?" he said as Parker joined him.

"Hoffa!" Parker slapped his staff hard against the palm of his left hand. "He really needles me, that one."

"What did he do?"

"Dumb insolence we'd have called it in the Guards."

"That's an Army charge—it won't wash here," Hagen pointed out.

"I know that only too damned well." Parker leaned against the bonnet of the Land-Rover, a muscle twitching in his right cheek. "It doesn't help matters when every con in the place treats him like Lord God Almighty."

"He's a big man in their book."

"Not in mine, he isn't. Just another cheap crook."

"Hardly that." Hagen laughed gently. "Nine hundred thousand quid is quite a bundle by anyone's standards and not a sou of it recovered—remember that."

"And what did it buy him?" Parker demanded. "Five years behind bars and another fifteen to go. That really must have taken genius."

"Poor old Ben." Hagen grinned. "He put too much trust in a woman. A lot of good men have made that mistake before him."

Parker exploded angrily. "Now you're sticking up for him for God's sake."

The smile was wiped from Hagen's face as if by an invisible hand and when he replied, there was steel in his voice. "Not exactly, but I do try to understand him which is a major part of my job.

Yours too, though that fact seems to have escaped your notice so far." Before the younger man could reply he glanced at his watch and added, "Three o'clock. We'll have them in for tea if you please, Mr. Parker."

He turned and walked a few paces away, the Alsatian at his heels and Parker stood there glaring after him. After a moment or two, he seemed to gain some sort of control, took his whistle from his pocket and blew a shrill blast.

Below in the quarry Hoffa dropped his hammer and O'Brien straightened. "Not before time," he said and picked up his shirt.

From all parts of the quarry prisoners converged on the track and climbed towards the Land-Rovers where Parker was waiting to dispense tea from an urn which stood in the back of one of the vehicles. Each man picked up a mug from a pile at one side and moved past him and Hagen and half a dozen other officers stood in a group lighting cigarettes

Hoffa took his tea, ignoring Parker completely, gazing towards the horizon where a couple of helicopters had swung into view. He moved to join O'Brien who was watching them intently.

"Now wouldn't it be the grand thing if they'd drop in kind of unexpected like and whisk us away," the Irishman observed.

Hoffa watched the helicopters drift across the distant hills and shook his head. "Not a chance, Paddy. They're Army Air Corps. Augusta-Bell scout 'copters. They only take the pilot and one passenger. You'd need something a little more substantial."

O'Brien swallowed some of his tea and made a

wry face. "I wonder what they make it with—turpentine?"

Hoffa didn't reply. He watched the helicopters disappear over the horizon and turned to Hagen who stood a couple of yards away talking to another officer.

"Could I have the time, Mr. Hagen?"

"Thinking of going somewhere, Ben?" Hagen demanded good-humouredly and there was general laughter.

"You never know."

Hagen glanced at his watch. "Three-fifteen."

Hoffa nodded his thanks, gazed down at the contents of the enamel mug in his right hand for a moment and then walked towards the Land-Rover where Parker still stood beside the tea urn.

He frowned warily as Hoffa approached and held out the mug. "Would you mind telling me what this is supposed to be, Mr. Parker, sir?" he said mildly.

Behind him, the voices died away and Hagen called sharply, "What's all this then, Hoffa?"

Hoffa replied without turning round, "A simple enough question, Mr. Hagen." He held the mug out towards Parker. "Have you tasted it, Mr. Parker?"

"Have I hell," Parker said and the knuckles of his right hand showed white as he tightened his grip on his staff.

"Then I really think you should," Hoffa said gently and tossed the contents of the mug into Parker's face.

There was a moment of stunned silence and then everything seemed to happen at once. Parker moved in with a cry of rage, his staff flailing down and Hoffa ducked under it, doubled him over with a fist to the stomach and raised a knee into the decending face.

Behind him there was a roar of excitement from the other prisoners and a moment later, he was on the ground, borne down by a rush of officers. There was a brief struggle and he was jerked to his feet, wrists handcuffed in front of him.

The Alsatian snarled on the end of its steel chain, driving the excited prisoners back. Hagen shouting for order. He got it in the end, turned and came toward Hoffa, a slight, puzzled frown on his face, all the instinct, all the experience of thirty hard years telling him that there was something wrong here.

"You bloody fool," he said softly. "Six months' remission gone and for what?"

Hoffa gazed past him stolidly, face impassive, and Hagen shrugged and turned to Parker who leaned against the Land-Rover, blood on his face. "Are you all right?"

"My nose is broken."

"Think you could drive?"

Parker nodded, a handkerchief to his face. "I don't see why not."

Hagen turned to one of the other officers. "I'm leaving you in charge, Mr. Smith. Get them working and no nonsense. I expect to see some sweat when I get back."

The prisoners were marched away and Hagen slipped the Alsatian's lead. The dog moved across to Hoffa, sniffing at his boots, and Hagen said, "Let's have you then. Into the back of the green Land-Rover. Any funny stuff and I'll put the dog on you—that's a promise."

Hoffa moved across the Land-Rover without a word, the Alsatian at his heels. He climbed inside, sat on one of the benches and waited. A moment later Hagen joined him, closing and locking the rear door.

A small glass window gave a view of the interior of the cab. Parker's face appeared momentarily, the brief glance he gave Hoffa full of venom. He nodded to Hagen and a moment later, the engine roared into life and they drove away.

As the Land-Rover turned on to the dirt road that led across the moor, Hagen leaned across, a frown on his face. "All right, Ben, what's it all about?"

But Hoffa ignored him, gazing past his shoulder through the side window across the moors, his face calm and impassive. In some strange way it was as if he was waiting for something.

Somewhere to the east of them gunfire rumbled again and the brief ominous chatter of a machine gun was answered by sporadic shooting. Hagen glanced out of the side window and saw the red berets of the paratrooopers moving across a hillside two or three miles away. Another scout helicopter drifted across the horizon and the Alsatian growled uneasily. He ran a hand along its broad flank and patted it gently.

"Only a game, boy, only a game."

As the dog subsided, there was a sudden roar of an engine in the west and another helicopter lifted over the hillside and swept in towards the road. For a moment it kept pace with them, so close that he could read the code name painted on its side in white letters. The hatch was open and a soldier crouched there looking out, his green beret a splash of vivid colour.

"Look like commandos," Hagen said.

To his surprise, Hoffa answered him. "Sibe-Martin troop carrier. They can manage a dozen men and equipment. They've been using them in Borneo lately."

The commando waved and the helicopter swung ahead of them, lifted over a rise and disappeared.

Hagen turned to face Hoffa. "You seem to know your stuff."

"There was an article in *Globe* magazine last month," Hoffa said. "It's in the library."

Hagen shook his head and sighed. "You're a funny bloke, Ben. I never could figure you out and that's a fact."

Unexpectedly Hoffa smiled, immediately looking about ten years younger. "That's what my old man used to say. Too late now though. Too late for all of us."

"I suppose you're right."

Hagen reached for his cigarettes and as he got them out, the Land-Rover went over the rise and started down a heavily wooded valley. He gave a sudden exclamation and leaned forward. The helicopter had landed in a clearing at the edge of the trees and half a dozen commandos were strung out across the road.

The cab window was pushed back and Parker called, "What in the hell's all this then?"

"God knows," Hagen said. "Maybe they think we're on the other side."

Parker started to slow as a young officer walked forward, waving him down. Like his men, he wore a

combat jacket and his face was darkened with camouflage cream. As the Land-Rover rolled to a halt,
the rest of the party moved in on the run, tough,
determined looking men, each carrying a machine
pistol.

Parker opened the door of the cab and leaned out.
"Look, what is this?"

Hagen couldn't see what happened, but Parker
cried out in alarm, there was the sound of a scuffle,
a blow and then silence.

Boots crunched the dirt surface of the road as
someone walked round the side of the vehicle. A
moment later, the glass window at the top of the
rear door was shattered and the young officer
peered inside.

"All out," he said pleasantly. "This is the end of
the line."

Hagen glanced across at Hoffa, taking in the
smile on his face, realising that the whole affair had
been rigged from the start and the Alsatian leapt for
the broken window, a growl rising in its throat. For
a moment it stayed there, rearing up on its hind
legs trying to force its way through, and then the
top of its skull disintegrated in a spray of blood and
bone as someone shot it through the head.

The dog flopped back on the floor and the young
officer smiled through the window at them, gently
tapping his right cheek with the barrel of a .38 automatic.

"Now don't let's have any more fuss, old man,"
he said to Hagen pleasantly. "We're pushed for
time as it is."

Hagen looked across at Hoffa, despair on his face.

"You'll never get away with this, Ben. All you'll collect is another ten years."

"I wouldn't count on that," Hoffa said. "Now make it easy on yourself, Jack. These blokes mean business."

Hagen hesitated for only a moment longer and then he sighed. "All right—it's your funeral."

He took the keys from his pocket, moved to the door and unlocked it. He was immediately pulled outside and Hoffa followed him. Parker was lying on his face unconscious, wrists handcuffed behind his back.

From then on the whole affair rushed to its climax with the same military precision that had been a characteristic of the entire operation. Someone unlocked Hoffa's handcuffs and transferred them to Hagen while someone else gagged him with a strip of surgical tape. Parker's unconscious body had already been lifted into the rear of the Land-Rover and Hagen was pushed in after him. The door closed, the key turned in the lock with a grim finality.

There was blood on his face from the dead Alsatian and as he rolled away from it in disgust, swallowing the bile that rose in his throat, the Land-Rover started to move, lurching over the rough ground away from the road. Through the side window above his head he was aware of the trees as they moved into the wood, crashing through heavy undergrowth and then the vehicle braked suddenly so that he was thrown forward, striking his head against the wall.

He lay there fighting the darkness that threatened to drown him, a strange roaring in his ears. It was a minute or so before he realised it was the helicopter taking off again and by the time he had managed to scramble to his knees and slump down on to the bench, the sound was already fading into the distance.

It was fifteen minutes later and thirty miles on the side of the moor, when the helicopter put down briefly in a clearing in a heavily wooded valley. Hoffa and the young officer jumped to the ground and the helicopter lifted into the sky again and flew away to the west.

Hoffa was dressed as a hiker in denim pants and green quilted anorak, a rucksack slung over one shoulder and the young officer wore an expensive grey flannel suit. Minus the camouflage cream, his face was pale and rather aristocratic and he had about him the air of a man who has long since decided that life is obviously a rather bad joke and not to be taken seriously.

"How long have we got?" Hoffa demanded.

His companion shrugged. "An hour—two if we're lucky. It depends how soon the party at the quarry notice how long it's taking the Principal Officer to return."

"Is an hour long enough?"

"Certainly, but it won't be if we hang around here much longer."

"All right," Hoffa said. "Just one more thing— what do I call you?"

"Anything you like, old man." He grinned amiably. "What about Smith? Yes, I think I'd like that. I've always wondered what it must be like to be called Smith."

"And where in the hell did the Baron pick you up?" Hoffa asked.

Smith smiled again. "You'd be surprised, old man. You really would."

He led the way across the clearing into the wood, following a narrow path through the trees which later joined a broad dirt track. A few yards further on they came to a derelict water mill beside a stream and in a courtyard at the rear behind a broken wall, a black Zodiac was parked. A moment later they were driving away, bumping over the rutted track, finally energing into a narrow country road.

"Let's get one thing clear," Smith said as he changed into top gear and drove rapidly away. "We'll be together in this car for approximately forty minutes. If anything goes wrong, you're a hitch-hiker and I've never seen you before in my life."

"All right," Hoffa said. "Where do we go from here?"

"All in good time. We've some business to settle first."

"I was wondering when you'd get round to it."

"Hardly likely to forget a thing like that. Your share of the Peterfield Airport Robbery was exactly £320,000. Where is it?"

"How do I know I'm going to get a fair shake?" Hoffa demanded.

"Now don't start that sort of nonsense, old man. The Baron can't stand welshers. We've kept our part of the bargain—we've got you out. You tell us where the cash is and that completes what we call

Phase One of the operation. Once we've got our hands on the money, we can start Phase Two."

"Which includes getting me out of the country?"

"With a new identity nicely documented, plus half the money. I'd say that was a fair exchange for twenty years on the Moor."

"How can I be sure?"

"You'd better be, old man. You aren't going to get very far on your own."

"You've got a point there. Okay—the money's in a steamer trunk at Prices' Furniture Repository, Pimlico, in the name of Henry Walker."

Smith gave him a look of blank amazement. "You must be joking."

"Why should I? They specialise in clients who are going overseas for a lengthy period. I paid five years in advance. Even if it isn't collected on time it's safe enough. They've got to hang on to it for ten years before they can do anything—that's the law."

"Is there a receipt?"

"You won't get it without one."

"Who has it?"

"Nobody—it's at my mother's place in Kentish Town. You'll find an old Salvation Army Bible amongst my gear. The receipt's hidden in the spine. Fair enough?"

"It should be. I'll pass the information along."

"And what happens to me?"

"You'll be taken care of. If everything goes according to plan they'll start Phase Two, but not before the Baron has seen the colour of your money."

"Who is the Baron anyway? Anyone I know?"

"That sort of question just isn't healthy, old

man." Smith shrugged and for the first time, the slight, characteristic smile was not in evidence. "You may meet him eventually—you may not. I honestly wouldn't know."

The rest of the journey was passed in silence until twenty minutes later when they arrived at a cross-roads and he slowed to a halt. "This is where we part company."

On either hand the main road was visible for a good quarter of a mile, a narrow ribbon of asphalt falling across wild and rugged uplands. It was completely deserted and Hoffa frowned.

"What happens now?"

"Stand at the edge of the road like any normal hitch-hiker and you'll be picked up in approximately ten minutes if our man's on time."

"What's he driving?"

"I haven't the slightest idea. His opening words will be: 'Is there anywhere in particular you'd like me to take you?' You must answer: Babylon."

"For God's sake, what is all this?" Hoffa demanded angrily. "Some sort of game?"

"Depends how you look at it, doesn't it, old man? He'll tell you Babylon's too far for him, but he can take you part of the way."

"Then what happens?"

"I wouldn't know." He leaned across the opened the door. "On your way, there's a good chap and the best of British luck to you."

A moment later Hoffa found himself standing at the side of the road a bewildered frown on his face, the Zodiac a fast-dwindling noise in the distance.

It was quiet after a while, the only sound the wind whispering through the long grass and a cloud passed across the face of the sun so that suddenly it was cold and he shivered. There was a desperate air of unreality to everything and the events of the afternoon seemed to form part of some privileged nightmare.

He checked the watch Smith had given him on the helicopter. An hour and ten minutes since the ambush of the Land-Rover. From now on anything might happen. There was sweat on his forehead in spite of the cool breeze and he wiped it away with the back of his hand. What if some well-meaning farmer drove by and decided to offer him a lift? What was he going to say?

Somewhere in the distance, an engine sounded faintly and when he turned to look, a vehicle came over the crest of the hill. As it approached he saw that it was a tanker, a great six-wheeler, its body painted a brilliant red and it rolled to a halt beside him.

The driver leaned out of the cab and looked down, a craggy-faced man of sixty or so in an old flying jacket and tweed cap, a grey stubble covering his chin. For a long moment there was silence and then he said with a pronounced Scottish accent, "Is there anywhere in particular you'd like me to take you?"

"Babylon," Hoffa told him and the breath went out of him in a long sigh of relief.

"Well, now, that's a step too far for me, but I can take you part of the way."

He opened the door and stepped on to a ladder that gave access to the filling point on top of the tanker. To one side was a steel plate about two feet square painted black which carried the legend:

Danger—Handle with care—Hydrochloric Acid. He felt for a hidden catch at the base of the plate and it swung open.

Hoffa climbed up and peered inside. The compartment was about eight feet by three with a mattress as its base and he nodded briefly. "How long?"

"Six hours," the driver said. "No light, I'm afraid, and you can't smoke, but there's coffee in the thermos and some sandwiches in a biscuit tin. Best I can do."

"Can I ask you where we're going?"

The driver shook his head, face impassive. "Not in the contract, that one."

"All right," Hoffa said. "Let's get rolling."

He went through the hatch head-first and as he turned to face the light, the cover clanged into place, plunging him into darkness. Panic moved inside him and his throat went dry and then the tanker started to roll forward and the mood passed. He lay back on the mattress, head pillowed on his hands and after a while his eyes closed and he slept.

At that precise moment some ten miles away, the man who had called himself Smith braked to a halt in the High Street of the first village he came to, went into a public telephone box and dialled a London number.

A woman answered him, her voice cool and impersonal. "Worldwide Exports Ltd."

"Simon Vaughan speaking from the West Country."

The voice didn't change. "Nice to hear from you. How are things down there?"

"Couldn't be better. Our client's on his way. Anything on the news yet?"

"Not a murmur."

"The lull before the storm. You'll find the goods in a steamer trunk at Price's Furniture Repository, Pimlico, in the name of Henry Walker. The receipt's in the spine of an old Salvation Army Bible amongst his gear at his mother's place in Kentish Town. I shouldn't think a nice young lady welfare officer would have too much trouble in getting that out of her."

"I'll handle it myself."

"I wouldn't waste too much time. It's almost five o'clock. The furniture repository probably closes at six. Might be an idea to give them a ring, just to make sure they'll stay open for you."

"Leave it to me. You've done well. He'll be pleased."

"Anything to oblige, old girl, that's me."

Vaughan replaced the receiver and lit a cigarette, a slight far-away look in his eyes. "Oh, what I'd like to do to you, sweetie," he murmured softly and as he returned to the car, there was a smile on his face.

Hoffa came awake slowly and lay staring through the heavy darkness, trying to work out where he was and then he remembered and pushed himself up on one elbow. According to the luminous dial on his watch it was a quarter past ten which meant they had been on the go for a little over five hours. Not much longer to wait and he lay back again, head pillowed on his hands, thinking of many things, but in particular of how he was going to start to live again—really live, in some place of warmth and light where the sun always shone and every woman was beautiful.

He was jerked out of his reverie as the tanker braked and started to slow. It rolled to a halt, but the engine wasn't turned off. The hatch opened and the driver's face appeared, a pale mask against the night sky.

"Out you get!"

It was a fine night with stars strung away to the horizon, but there was no moon. Hoffa stood at the side of the road stretching to ease his cramped limbs as the driver dropped the hatch back into place.

"What now?"

"You'll find a track leading up the mountain on the other side of the road. Wait there. Someone will pick you up."

He was inside the cab before Hoffa could reply, there was a hiss of air as he released the brake and the tanker rolled away into the night. Hoffa watched the red tail lights fade into darkness, then picked up his rucksack and moved across the road.

He found the track without any difficulty and stood there peering into the darkness, wondering what to do next. The voice, when it came, made him start in alarm because of its very unexpectedness.

"Is there anywhere in particular you'd like me to take you?"

It was a woman who had spoken—a woman with a pronounced Yorkshire accent and he peered forward trying to see her as he replied, "Babylon."

"Too far for me, but I can take you part of the way."

She moved close, her face a pale blur in the darkness, then turned without another word and walked away. Hoffa followed her, the loose stones of the track rattling under his feet. In spite of his long sleep, he was tired. It had, after all, been quite a day and somewhere up ahead there had to be food and a bed.

They walked for perhaps half a mile, climbing all the time and he was aware of hills on either side of them and the cold chill in the wind and then the track turned a shoulder and below in a hollow beside a stream was a farmhouse, a light in the downstairs window.

A dog barked hollowly as she pushed open a five-barred gate and led the way across the cobbled yard. As they approached the front door, it opened suddenly and a man stood there framed against the light, a shotgun in his hands.

"You found him then, Molly?"

For the first time Hoffa had a clear view of the girl and realised with a sense of surprise, that she couldn't have been more than nineteen or twenty years of age with haunted eyes and a look that said she hadn't smiled in a long time.

"Will you want me for anything more tonight?" she said in a strange dead voice.

"Nay, lass, off you go to bed and look in on your mother. She's been asking for you."

The girl slipped past him and he leaned a shotgun against the wall and came forward, hand outstretched. "A real pleasure, Mr. Hoffa. I'm Sam Crowther."

"So you know who I am?" Hoffa said.

"They've been talking about nowt else on the radio all night."

"Any chance of finding out where I am?"

Crowther chuckled. "Three hundred and fifty miles from where you started off. They won't be looking for you round here, you may be certain of that."

"Which is something, I supppose," Hoffa said. "What happens now? Do we move into Phase Two yet?"

"I had a telephone call from London no more than an hour ago. Everything went as smooth as silk. You'll have no worries from now on, Mr. Hoffa." He turned and called over his shoulder, "Billy—where are you, Billy? Let's be having you."

The man who appeared in the doorway was a giant. At least six feet four in height, he had the shoulders and arms of an ape and a great lantern jaw. He grinned foolishly, a dribble of saliva oozing from the corner of his mouth as he shambled into the yard and Crowther clapped him on the shoulder.

"Good lad, Billy, let's get moving. There's work to be done." He turned and smiled. "This way, Mr. Hoffa."

He led the way across the yard, Hoffa at his heels, Billy bringing up the rear and opened a gate leading into a small courtyard. The only thing it seemed to contain was an old well surrounded by a circular brick wall about three feet high.

Hoffa took a step forward. "Now what?"

His reply was a single stunning blow from the rear delivered with such enormous power that his spine snapped like a rotten stick.

He lay there writhing on the ground and Crowther stirred him with the toe of his boot. "In he goes, Billy."

Hoffa was still alive as he went headfirst into the well. His body bounced from the brickwork twice on the way down, but he could feel no pain. Strangely enough, his last conscious thought was that Hagen had been right. It had been his funeral after all and then the cold waters closed over him and he plunged into darkness.

2

Cops and Robbers

When the noon whistle blew a steady stream of workers began to emerge from Lonsdale Metals. In the café opposite the main gates Paul Chavasse got to his feet, folded his newspaper and went outside. It was precisely this busy period that he had been waiting for and he crossed the road quickly

The main entrance itself was blocked by a swing bar which was not raised until any outgoing vehicle had been checked by the uniformed guard, but the workers used a side gate and crowded through it slowly to a chorus of ribald comments and good humoured laughter.

Undistinguishable from the rest of them in brown overalls and tweed cap, Chavasse plunged into the crowd, working against the stream. He met with some good natured abuse as he forced his way through, but a moment later he was inside the gate. He moved through the crowd, glancing quickly through the window of the gatehouse on his left, noting the three uniformed security guards at the table, coffee and sandwiches spread before them, an Alsatian squatting in the corner.

The workers were still moving towards the gate in a steady stream and Chavasse passed through them quickly, crossed the yard to the main block and entered the basement garage. He had spent the previous night poring over the plans S2 had provided until the layout of the building was so impressed on his mind that he was able to move with perfect confidence.

There were still one or two mechanics about, but he ignored them, mounted the ramp, walked behind the line of waiting vehicles parked in the loading bay and pressed the button for the service lift. A moment later he was on his way to the third floor.

It was strangely quiet when he stepped out and he paused, listening, before moving along the corridor. The door to the wages office was on the third from the end and marked *Private*. He glanced at it briefly in passing, turned the corner and opened a door which carried the sign *Fire Exit*. Concrete stairs dropped into a dark well beneath him and on the wall to his left he found what he was looking for—a battery of fuse boxes.

Each box was numbered neatly in white paint. He pushed the handle on number ten into the off position and returned to the corridor.

He knocked on the door of the wages office and waited. This was the crucial moment. According to his information, the staff went to lunch between noon and one o'clock leaving only the chief cashier on duty, but nothing was certain in this life—he had learned that if nothing else in seven years of working for the Bureau and there were bound to be days when someone or other decided to have sandwiches instead of going out. Two he could handle—any more than that and he was in trouble. Not that it mattered—it all came down to the same thing in the end and he smiled wryly. On the other hand it might be amusing to see just how far he could go.

A spyhole flicked open in front of him and he caught the glint of an eye.

"Mr. Crabtree?" Chavasse said. "I'm from Maintenance. There's been a partial power failure on this floor and I'm checking each office to find the cause. Is everything all right here, sir?"

"Just a moment." The cover of the spyhole dropped into place. A moment later there was the rattle of a chain, the door opened and a small white haired man peered out. "The lights don't seem to be working at all. You'd better come in."

Chavasse stepped inside, noting in that first quick moment that they were alone and Crabtree busied himself in locking and chaining the door again. He was perhaps sixty and wore neat gold-rimmed spectacles. When he turned and found the muzzle of a .38 automatic staring him in the face, his eyes widened in horror, his shoulders sagging so that he seemed to shrink and become visibly smaller.

Chavasse stifled a pang of remorse and tapped him gently on the cheek with the barrel of the automatic. "Do as you're told and you'll come out of this in one piece—understand?" Crabtree nodded dumbly and Chavasse produced a pair of handcuffs from a pocket in his overalls and gestured to a chair. "Sit down and put your hands behind you."

He handcuffed Crabtree quickly, secured his ankles with a length of cord and squatted in front of him. "Comfortable?"

The cashier seemed to have made a remarkable recovery and smiled thinly. "Relatively."

Chavasse warmed to him. "Your wage bill here runs you between forty and fifty thousand pounds depending on the amount of overtime worked. What's the figure this week?"

"Forty-five thousand," Crabtree replied without the slightest hesitation. "Or to put it another way, just over half a ton dead weight. Somehow I don't think you're going to get very far."

Chavasse grinned. "We'll see, shall we?"

There was money everywhere, some of it stacked in neat bundles as it had come from the bank, a large amount already made up into wage packets in wooden trays. The strongroom door stood open and inside he found a trolley with canvas sides containing several large money bags which, from their weight, held silver and copper. He removed the bags quickly, wheeled the trolley into the office and pushed it along the line of desks, sweeping in bundles of banknotes and wage packets together. Crabtree was right—it added up to quite a load yet it took him no more than three minutes to clear the lot.

He pushed the trolley to the door and Crabtree said, "I don't know if you're aware of it, but we do a great deal of work for the RAF here so our security system's rather special."

"I got in, didn't I?"

"But not while you were pushing half a ton of banknotes in front of you and it's impossible for any vehicle to get through that gate until it's been thoroughly checked. Something of a problem, I should have thought."

"Sorry I haven't time to discuss it now," Chavasse said. "But don't fail to buy an evening paper. They've promised to print the solution for me."

He produced a large piece of sticking plaster and pasted it over the cashier's mouth before he could reply. "Can you breathe all right?" Crabtree nodded, something strangely like regret in his eyes, and Chavasse grinned. "It's been fun. Somehow I don't think you'll be on your own for long."

The door closed behind him with a click and Crabtree sat there in the silence, waiting, feeling more alone than at any other time in his life. It seemed an age before he heard heavy feet pounding along the corridor and the anxious knocking started on the door.

The previous Wednesday when it all started, was a morning of bright sunshine and Chavasse had chosen to walk through the park on his way to Bureau headquarters. Life, for an intelligence agent, is a strange and rather haphazard existence compounded of short, often violent, periods of service in the field followed by months of comparative inactivity, often spent in routine antiespionage investigations or administration.

For almost half a year Chavasse had clocked in each morning as ordered, to sit behind a desk in a converted attic in the old house in St. John's Wood to spend the day sifting through reports from field sections in all parts of the globe—demanding, highly important work that had to be done thoroughly or not at all—and so damned boring.

But the sun was out, the sky was blue, the dresses were shorter than he'd ever known them, so that for once he took his time and strolled across the grass between the trees smoking a cigarette, discovering and not for the first time in his life, that after all, a man didn't need a great deal to be utterly and completely happy—for the moment, at any rate. Somewhere a clock struck eleven. He glanced at his watch, swore softly and hurried towards the main road.

It was almost half past the hour when he went up the steps of the house in St. John's Wood and pressed the bell beside the brass plate that carried the legend *Brown & Co—Importers and Exporters*.

After a few moments, the door was opened by a tall greying man in a blue serge uniform and Chavasse hurried past him. "I'm late this morning, George."

George looked worried. "Mr. Mallory was asking for you. Miss Frazer's been phoning down every five minutes for the past hour."

Chavasse was already half-way up the curving Regency staircase, a slight flicker of excitement moving inside him. If Mallory wanted him urgently, then it had to be for something important. With any kind of luck at all the pile of reports that overflowed from his in-tray were going to have to be passed on to someone else. He moved along the landing quickly and opened the white-painted door at the far end.

Jean Frazer turned from a filing cabinet, a small, attractive woman of thirty who wore a red woollen dress of deceptively simple cut that made the best of her rather full figure. She removed her heavy library spectacles and shook her head.

"You would, wouldn't you?"

Chavasse grinned. "I went for a walk in the park. The sun was shining, the sky was blue and I seemed to see unattached young females everywhere."

"You must be getting old," she said and picked up the telephone.

"Oh, I wouldn't say that. Skirts are shorter than ever. I was often reminded of you."

A dry, remote voice cut in on them. "What is it?"

"Mr. Chavasse is here, Mr. Mallory."

"Send him in. No calls for the next hour."

She replaced the receiver and turned, a slight mocking smile on her mouth. "Mr. Mallory will see you now, sir."

"I love you too," Chavasse said and he crossed to the green baize door, opened it and went in.

"Prison escapes have always been a problem," Black said. "They never average less than two hundred and fifty a year."

"I must say that seems rather a lot." Mallory helped himself to a Turkish cigarette from the box on his desk.

Although by nature a kindly man, as a Detective Chief Superintendent with the special Branch at New Scotland Yard, Charlie Black was accustomed to his inferiors running to heed his slightest command. Indeed, there was a certain pleasure to be derived from the sudden nervousness noted in even the most innocent of individuals when they discovered who and what he was. But we are all creatures of our environment, moulded by everything and anything that has happened to us since the day we were born and Black, branded by the years spent below stairs in the mansion in Belgrave Square where his mother, widowed by the first world war, had been cook, stirred uneasily in his chair for he was in the presence of what she, God rest her soul, would have termed his betters.

It was all there—the grey flannel suit, the Old Etonian Tie, the indefinable aura of authority. Ridiculous, but for the briefest of moments, he might have been a small boy again returning the old Lord's dog after a walk in the park and receiving a pat on the head and sixpence.

He pulled himself together quickly. "It's not quite as bad as it looks. About a hundred and fifty men each year simply walk out of open prisons—nothing to stop them. I suppose you could argue that the selection procedure has been faulty in the first place. Another fifty are probably men released on parole for funerals and weddings and so on, who simply take off instead of coming back."

"Which leaves you with a hard core of about fifty genuine escapes a year."

"That's it—or was. During the past couple of years there's been an increase in the really spectacular sort of escape. I suppose it all started with Wilson the train robber's famous break from Birmingham. The first time a gang had actually broken into a prison to get someone out."

"Real commando stuff."

"And brilliantly executed."

"Which is where this character the Baron comes in?"

Black nodded. "To our certain knowledge he's been responsible for at least half a dozen big breaks during the past year or so. Added to that he runs an underground pipeline by which criminals in danger of arrest can flee the country. On two occasions we've managed to arrest minor members of his organisation—people who've passed on men we've been chasing to someone else."

"Have you managed to squeeze anything out of them?"

"Not a thing—mainly because they honestly hadn't anything to say. The pipeline seems to be organised on the Communist cell system, the one Resistance used in France during the war. Each member is concerned only with his own particular task. He may know the next step along the route, but no more than that. It means that if one individual is caught, the organisation as a whole is still safe."

"And doesn't anyone know who the Baron is?"

"The Ghost Squad have been trying to find out for more than a year now. They've got nowhere. One thing's certain—he isn't just another crook— he's something special. May even be a Continental."

Mallory had a file open on the desk in front of him. He examined it in silence for a moment and shook his head. "It looks to me as if your only hope of finding out anything about him at all would be to get a line on one of his future clients which in theory should be impossible. There must be something like sixty thousand men in gaol right now— how do you find out which one it is?"

"A simple process of elimination really. If there's

a pattern to his activities it's to be found in his choice of clientele. They've all been long term prisoners and have had considerable financial resources." Black opened a buff folder, took out a typed sheet of foolscap and a photo and passed them across. "Have a look at the last one."

Mallory examined it for a moment and nodded. "Ben Hoffa—I remember this one. The affair on Dartmoor last month. A gang disguised as Royal Marine Commandos ambushed a prison vehicle during a military exercise and spirited him away. Any news of him since?"

"Not a word. Hoffa and two confederates, George Saxton and Harry Youngblood were serving sentences of twenty years apiece for the Peterfield Airport robbery. Do you remember it?"

"I can't say I do."

"It was five years ago now. They hi-jacked a Northern Airways Dakota which was carrying just under a million pounds in old notes, a special consignment from the Central Scottish Bank to the Bank of England in London. A beautiful job. I have to admit that. Only the three of them involved and they got clean away."

"What went wrong?"

"Hoffa had the wrong kind of girl friend. She decided she'd rather have the £10,000 reward the Central Banks were offering than Ben and his share of the loot plus an uncertain future."

"And the money was never recovered?"

"Not one farthing." Black handed across another photo. "That's George Saxton. He escaped from Grange End last year. It was a carbon copy of the Wilson affair. Half a dozen men broke-in under cover of darkness and actually brought him out. Not a word of him since then. As far as we're concerned he might as well have ceased to exist."

"Which leaves Youngblood presumably?"

"Only just or I miss my guess," Black said grimly and pushed another file across.

The face that stared up from the photo was full of intelligence and a restless animal vitality, one corner of the mouth lifted in a slight mocking smile. Mallory was immediately interested and quickly read through the details on the attached sheet.

Harry Youngblood was forty-two years of age and had joined the Navy in 1941 at the age of seventeen, finishing the war as a petty officer in motor torpedo boats. After the war he had continued in the same line of work, but on more unorthodox lines and in 1949 was sentenced to eighteen months imprisonment for smuggling. A charge of conspiracy to rob the mails had been dropped for lack of evidence in 1952. Between then and his final conviction in May 1961 he had served no further terms of imprisonment, but had been questioned by the police on no fewer than thirty-one occasions in connection with indictable offences.

"Quite a character," Mallory said. "He seems to have tried his hand at just about everything in the book."

"To be honest with you, I always had a sneaking regard for him myself and I don't usually have much time for sentimentality where villains are concerned. If he'd taken another turning after the war instead of that smuggling caper, things might have been very different."

"And now he's doing twenty years?"

"That's the theory. We're not too happy about what might happen considering the way his two confederates have gone. He's at Fridaythorpe now under maximum security, but there's a limit to how harshly he can be treated anyway. He had a slight stroke about three months ago."

Mallory glanced at the photo again. "I must say he looks healthy enough to me. Are you sure it was genuine?"

"An electroencephalograph can't lie," Black said. "And it definitely indicated severe disturbance to wave patterns in the brain. Another thing—you can apparently simulate a heart attack by using drugs, but not a stroke. He was very thoroughly checked. They had him in Manningham General Infirmary for three days."

"Wasn't that dangerous? I should have thought it a perfect situation for someone to break him out."

Black shook his head. "He was unconscious most of the time. They had him in the enclosed ward with two prison officers at his side night and day."

"Couldn't he be treated at the prison?"

"They haven't the facilities. Like most gaols, Fridaythorpe has a sick bay and a visiting doctor. Anything serious is treated in the enclosed ward of the local hospital. If a prisoner is likely to be ill for an extended period he's transferred to the prison hospital at Wormwood Scrubs. That doesn't apply to Youngblood with a complaint like his. In any case the Home Office would never sanction his transfer. The very fact that it's a hospital means that it can't possibly offer maximum security. They'd be frightened to death that one of the

London gangs might seize their opportunity to try to break him out."

Mallory lit another cigarette, got to his feet and walked to the window. "All very interesting. Of course the Commissioner sent me a very full report, but I must say your personal account has clarified one or two things." He turned, frowning reflectively. "As I see it, it all boils down to one thing. You want us to supply you with an operative. Someone who could be introduced into prison in the normal way and who, at least in theory, might be able to win Youngblood's confidence. Why can't you use one of your own men?"

"Most crooks can spot a copper a mile away—just one of those things and it works both ways, of course. That's why the Commissioner thought of your organisation, sir. You see the man we need for this job wouldn't last five minutes if there was even a hint that he wasn't a crook himself so his personal attitude and temperament would be of primary importance."

"What you're really saying is that my operatives have what might be termed the criminal mind, Superintendent?" Black looked slightly put out and Mallory shook his head. "You're quite right. They wouldn't last long in the field if they hadn't."

"You think you could find us someone?"

Mallory nodded, sat down at his desk and looked at the file again. "Oh yes, I think we can manage that. As it happens I have someone available who should be more than suitable." He flicked the switch on the intercom and said sharply, "Any sign of Chavasse yet?"

"I'm afraid not, Mr. Mallory," Jean Frazer said.

"Chavasse?" Black said. "Sounds foreign."

"His father was a French officer killed during the last war. His mother is English. She raised the boy over here. You might say he's traveled extensively since."

Black hesitated and said carefully, "He'll need all his wits about him for this one, Mr. Mallory."

"As it happens, he has a Ph.D. in Modern Languages, Superintendent," Mallory answered a trifle frostily, "and he was once a lecturer at one of our older universities. Is that good enough for you?"

Black's jaw went slack. "Then how in the hell did he get into this game?"

"An old story. The important thing is why does he stay?" Mallory shrugged. "I suppose you could say he has a flair for our sort of work and, when called upon, he doesn't hesitate to squeeze the trigger. Most human beings do you know." He smiled thinly. "Come to think of it, I don't think you would approve of him at all."

Black looked rather stunned. "To be perfectly frank, sir, he sounds as if he should be behind bars to me."

"Rather an apt comment under the circumstances."

A moment later the intercom buzzed and Jean Frazer announced Chavasse.

He paused just inside the door. "Sorry I'm late, sir," he said to Mallory.

"Never mind that now. I'd like you to meet Detective Chief Superintendent Black of the Special Branch. He'd like you to go to prison for a few months."

"Now that sounds interesting," Chavasse said and he moved forward to shake hands.

He was a shade under six feet with good shoulders and moved with the grace of the natural athlete, but it was the face which was the most interesting feature. It was handsome, even aristocratic—the kind that could have belonged equally to the professional soldier or scholar and the heritage of his Breton father was plain to see in the high cheek-bones. As he shook hands, his face was illuminated by a smile of great natural charm, but thirty years of police work had taught Charlie Black the importance of eyes. These were dark and strangely remote and remembering what Mallory had said, he shivered slightly, suddenly feeling completely out of his depth. Straightforward police work was one thing, but this. . . .

He heard Mallory's next words with an almost audible sigh of relief. "I think we can manage from here on in, Superintendent. Many thanks for coming. As I said before, you've clarified several things for me. You can tell the Commissioner I'll be in touch later in the day. Miss Frazer will see you out."

He put on his glasses and started to examine the file in front of him again. Black got to his feet awkwardly, started to put out his hand and thought better of it. He nodded to Chavasse and went out rather quickly.

Chavasse chuckled. "God bless the British bobby."

Mallory glanced up at him. "Who—Black? Oh, he's all right digging in his own patch."

"He was like some wretched schoolboy leaving

the headmaster's study—couldn't get out fast enough."

"Nonsense." Mallory tossed a file across to him. "I'll talk to you when you've read that."

He occupied himself with some other papers while Chavasse worked his way through the typed sheets and the documents from Criminal Records Office at the Yard.

After a while Mallory sat back. "Well, what do you think?"

"Could be interesting, but since when have you been so keen to help the police?"

"There are one or two things about this affair that the Yard don't know."

"Such as?"

"Remember what a stink there was last year when Henry Galbraith, the nuclear physicist who was serving fifteen years for passing information to the Chinese, escaped from Felversham Gaol?"

Chavasse nodded. "I must admit I was surprised at the time. Galbraith was hardly my idea of a man of action."

"He's turned up in Peking."

"You mean the Baron was behind that?" Mallory nodded and Chavasse whistled softly. "They must have paid plenty."

"On top of that on at least three occasions this year just when we've been about to close in on someone important who's been working for the other side, they've been spirited away. A Foreign Office type disappeared last month and turned up in Warsaw and I can tell you now, he knew too damned much. The Prime Minister was hopping mad about that one—he had to go to Washington the same week."

"Which all tells us something interesting about the Baron," Chavasse observed. "Whatever else he is, he's no patriot—just a hard-headed business-man."

He looked down at the file again and Mallory said, "What do you think?"

"About the general idea," Chavasse shrugged. "I am not too sure. I'm to go to gaol and share a cell with Harry Youngblood, that's about the size of it. Are you sure it can be arranged?"

Mallory nodded. "The Home Office could handle that part of it direct with the prison governor. He might not like it, but he'd have to do as he was told. He'd be the only one who would know. We'll fix you up with a new identity. Something nice and inter-esting. Ex-officer cashiered for embezzlement—recently deported from Brazil as an undesirable and so forth."

"It might be just a colossal waste of time, have you considered that?" Chavasse said. "It may seem logical that Harry Youngblood should be next for shaving, but it's far from certain."

Mallory shook his head. "I think it is. Take this slight stroke he's had—that's as fishy as hell. No previous history and he's always enjoyed perfect health."

"According to the report it was a genuine attack."

"I know and Black pointed out that a stroke can't be induced artifically by use of a drug."

"Is he wrong?"

"Let's say misinformed—officially there is no

such drug, but they have been experimenting with one in Holland for a year now. A thing called Mabofine. It disturbs the wave patterns in the brain in the same way as insulin or shock treatment. They hope to use it with mental patients."

"What you're really saying is that you suspect that some sort of plot is already in operation to get him out. What am I supposed to do? Find out what I can and stop him or try to go along for the ride?"

"It could be an interesting trip. It might lead us straight to the man we're looking for."

"Another thing—it might be a year or more before they move."

"And you don't fancy spending that long as a guest of Her Majesty?"

Chavasse tossed Youngblood's record card across the desk. "It's more than that. Look at that face—notice the eyes. To hell with those jolly newspaper stories about Harry Youngblood, the smuggler with the good war record—the modern Robin Hood with a heart of corn for a tale of woe. In my book he's a man with a mind like a cut-throat razor who'd sell his grandmother for cigarette money in the right situation. He'd smell me out as a phoney for sure. I wouldn't last a week and prisons can be dangerous places or hadn't you heard?"

"But what if he had to accept you? What if he didn't have any choice in the matter?"

Chavasse frowned. "I don't get it."

"All you have to do is pull the right job and get yourself five years. A reasonably spectacular hold-up for preference. Something that will spread your face all over the front page for a day or two."

"You're not asking much, are you?"

"Actually, I've already got something lined up," Mallory continued calmly. "I got it from one of our contacts at the Yard. Whenever they find a firm that isn't taking adequate security precautions, they step in and offer some sound advice. In this case it might have more effect coming from you. You'll have to let them catch you of course."

"Nice of you to put it that way. What if I show them a clean pair of heels?"

"An anonymous phone call to the Yard telling them where you are should do the trick." He smiled. "I'm sure Jean Frazer would enjoy handling that bit."

Chavasse sighed. "Well, I did say I wanted a little more action. What's the firm?"

Mallory opened another file and pushed it across. "Lonsdale Metals," he said.

The guard on the gate stretched and took a couple of paces towards the gatehouse, easing his cramped muscles. A long morning, but only ten minutes to go. He turned and a red works van shot out of the garage and roared across the yard, gears racing.

As he jumped forward in alarm, it skidded to a halt, the bonnet no more than a yard away from the swing bar that blocked the entrance. The young man who scrambled out of the cab looked considerably shocked and there was blood on his face. He lost his balance, falling to one knee and as the guard helped him to his feet he was joined by his three companions.

The driver seemed to have difficulty in speaking. He swallowed then flung out an arm dramatically in the general direction of the main block. "Wages office!" he managed to gasp.

He started to sag to the ground and the gate guard caught him quickly. "Better get up there fast," he said to the other three. "I'll get this lad inside and phone for the police."

They went across the yard on the run, the Alsatian at their heels and the gate guard tightened his grip around the van driver's shoulders. "You don't look too good. Come in and sit down."

The driver nodded, wiping blood from his face with the back of a hand and together, they moved into the gatehouse. The guard could never afterwards be quite sure about what happened next. He eased the driver into a chair and moved towards the desk. He was aware of no sound, but as he reached for the telephone was struck a stunning blow at the base of the skull that sent him crashing to the floor.

He lay there for a few moments, senses reeling, aware of the clang of the swing bar outside as it was raised, of the sudden roar of an engine as the van was driven rapidly away and then darkness flooded over him.

When Chavasse went up the stairs of the dingy house in Poplar and opened the door at the end of the landing, Jean Frazer was lying on the bed reading a magazine.

She swung her legs to the floor, a slight frown on her face. "Is that blood on your cheek?"

Chavasse wiped it away casually. "Something else entirely, I assure you."

"Did you get in?"

"And out again."

Her eyes widened. "With the money?"

He nodded. "It's downstairs in the yard in an old Ford van I bought this morning."

"Presumably the law isn't far behind?"

Chavasse moved to the window wiping his face with a towel and peered into the street. "I shouldn't think so. I switched vehicles miles away on the other side of the Thames. In fact if I hadn't shown my face around as much as I did, I've a shrewd suspicion I could have got away with this."

"Dangerous talk." She pulled on her shoes. "Seriously, Paul, how on earth did you manage it?"

"You know what the newsboys say? Read all about it. I wouldn't want to spoil your fun."

She sighed. "Ah, well, I suppose I'd better go and put in that call to Scotland Yard."

As she moved round the bed he pulled her into his arms. "I could be away for a hell of a long time, Jean," he said mockingly. "I don't suppose you'd care to give me something to remember you by."

She pulled down his head, kissed him once and disengaged herself. "The best I can do at the moment. I've got my Delilah bit to take care of. If Mallory lets me, I'll come and see you on visiting days."

The door closed behind her and Chavasse locked it. Nothing to do now except wait for them to come for him. He placed the automatic to hand on the locker by the window, lit a cigarette and lay down on the bed.

It was not more than twenty minutes later that he heard sounds of faint movement on the landing outside. There was a timid knock on the door and Mrs.

Clegg, the landlady, called, "Are you in, Mr. Drummond?"

"What do you want?" he said.

"There's a letter for you. Came while you were out."

"Just a minute."

He took a deep breath and unlocked the door. It smashed into him instantly and he was carried back across the bed which collapsed under the combined weight of four very large policemen.

He put up a semblance of a struggle, but a moment later handcuffs were snapped around his wrists and he was hauled to his feet. A large amiable looking man in a fawn gaberdine raincoat and battered Homburg paused in the doorway to light a cigarette, then moved in.

"All right, son, where's the loot?"

"Why don't you take a running jump?" Chavasse told him.

"Careful—you'll be making sounds like a man next."

There was a pounding on the stairs and a young constable entered the run. "We found it, inspector," he said, struggling for breath. "Back of an old Ford van in the yard."

The inspector turned to Chavasse and sighed. "Forty-five thousand quid and what bloody good has it done you?"

"I'll let you know," Chavasse said. "I'll have to think about it."

"You'll have plenty of time for that—'about seven years or I miss my guess." He nodded to the constables. "Go on, get him out of here."

Chavasse grinned impudently. "See you in court, inspector."

He was still laughing as they took him downstairs.

3

Maximum Security

The governor of Fridaythrope Gaol put down his
pen and switched on the desk lamp. It was just after
eight with darkness drawing in fast and he went to
the window and watched the last light of day touch
the rim of the hills across the valley with fire before
night fell.

There was a firm knock on the door and as he
turned, Atkinson, the Principal Officer, entered, a
large buff envelope in one hand.

"Sorry to bother you, sir, but the new man is
here—Drummond. You said you wanted to see him
personally."

The governor nodded and moved back to his
desk. "So I did. Is he outside?"

Atkinson nodded. "That's right, sir."

"What's he like?"

Atkinson shrugged. "A gentleman gone nasty if
you follow me." He opened the envelope and placed
the documents it contained in front of the governor.
"You'll remember the case, sir. It was in all the

papers at the time. Forty-five thousand and he almost got away with it."

"Didn't someone inform on him?"

"That's right, sir—an anonymous tip to the Yard, but he was going to seed long before that. He was a Captain in the Royal Engineers—cashiered for embezzlement seven or eight years ago. Since then he's been knocking around South America getting up to God knows what."

The Governor nodded. "Not a very pretty picture! Still—a man of some intelligence. I'm thinking of putting him in with Youngblood."

Atkinson was unable to conceal his surprise. "Might I ask why, sir?"

The governor leaned back in his chair. "Frankly, I'm worried about Youngblood—have been ever since he had that stroke. Sooner or later he'll have another—they always do—and he'll need specialised medical treatment very, very quickly. Can you imagine what would happen if he had such an attack in the middle of the night and died on us!"

"That's hardly likely, sir. He's checked every hour."

"A lot could happen in an hour. On the other hand, if someone was there all the time." He shook his head. "I'm certain a cell mate is the best answer from our point of view and this chap Drummond should do very nicely. Let's have a look at him."

The Principal Officer opened the door and stood to one side. "All right, lad," he barked. "Look lively now. Stand on the mat and give your name and number."

The prisoner moved into the room quickly and

stood on the rubber mat that was positioned exactly three feet away from the governor's desk.

"83278 Drummond, sir," Paul Chavasse said and waited at attention.

The light from the desk threw his face into relief. It had fined down in the past three months and the hair, close-cropped to the skull, gave him a strangely medieval appearance. He looked a thoroughly dangerous man and the governor frowned down at his records in some perplexity. This was not what he had expected—not at all what he had expected.

But then, the governor's paradox was that he knew nothing of prison life at all—what he saw each day was only the surface of a pond which Chavasse, in three short months, had plumbed to its depths in undergoing what was known in the legal profession as the due process of the law.

In the three months he had made seven separate court appearances and had already experienced the life of three different gaols. He had spent a month on remand in a place so primitive that the only sanitary arrangements in the cell consisted of an enamel pot. Each morning, he had formed one of the queue of men who shuffled along the landing to empty the nights slops into the single lavatory bowl at the end.

Prison Officers were now screws, men who like the rest of the humanity were good, bad and indifferent in about the usual proportions. There had been some who had treated him with decency and humanity, others who punctuated each command with the end of a staff jabbed painfully into the kidneys.

He had learned that there was little romance in crime—that most of his fellow prisoners were persistent offenders who could have made a better living if they had spent their lives in drawing the unemployment benefit. He had learned that murderers and rapists looked just like anyone else and that often the most masculine prisoners in appearance were sexual deviants.

Most important of all, like any jungle animal intent only on survival he had quickly acquired the customs and habits of his new surroundings so that he might fade into the background with the rest. And he had survived. He would never be quite the same man again, but he had survived.

"Six years." The governor looked up from the record card. "That means four if you keep out of trouble and earn full remission."

"Yes, sir."

The governor leaned back in his chair. "It's really quite distressing to see a man like you end up in this sort of a mess but I think we can help you. But you've got to help yourself as well, you know. Are you willing to try?"

Chavasse resisted a strong temptation to lean across the desk and smash his fist into the centre of that florid well-fed face and wondered whether the governor could possibly be putting on an act. On the other hand that was hardly likely—which must mean that he had accepted the introduction of an undercover agent into his establishment with the greatest reluctance.

"Anyway, you can best help yourself by helping me," the governor said. "I'm going to put you in with a man called Harry Youngblood. He's a long-term prisoner who suffered a stroke some time ago. Now the odds are that he might have another and it could be at night. If that happens I want you to ring for the Duty Officer at once. Speed is vital in these cases so I'm told. Do you understand?"

"Perfectly, sir."

"Youngblood works in the machine shop, doesn't he, Mr. Atkinson?"

"That's right, sir. Car number plates."

"Fine." The governor looked up at Chavasse again. "We'll put you in there for training and see how you like it. I'll follow your progress with interest."

He got to his feet as a sign that the interview was over and for the briefest of moments there was something in his eyes. It was as if he wanted to say something more, but couldn't think of the right words. In the end he nodded brusquely to the Principal Officer who led Chavasse out into the corridor.

The other gaols Chavasse had been in had been constructed during the reform era in the middle of the nineteenth century on a system commonly found in Her Majesty's Prisons of four three tiered cell blocks radiating like the spokes of a wheel from a central hall.

But Fridaythorpe was only two years old, a place of quiet and smooth concrete, air-conditioned and warmed by central heating with not a window to be seen.

They reached a central hall and entered a steel lift which rose ten floors before it halted. They stepped out on to a small concrete landing and

Chavasse could see a long white corridor stretching into the distance on the other side of a steel gate.

They stood there for a moment and then the gate opened smoothly and silently. They moved inside and it closed again.

"Impressed?" Atkinson demanded as Chavasse turned to examine it. "You're meant to be. It's operated electronically by remote control. The man who pressed the button is sitting in the control centre on the ground floor at the other end of the prison. He's one of a team of five who watch fifty-three television screens on a shift system twenty-four hours a day. You've been on view ever since we left the governor's office."

"Wonderful what you can do with science these days," Chavasse said.

"Nobody escapes from Fridaythorpe—just remember that," Atkinson said as they proceeded along the corridor. "Behave yourself and you'll get a square deal—try to act tough and you'll fall flat on your face."

He didn't seem to require an answer and Chavasse didn't attempt to give him one. They paused outside a door at the far end of the passage, Atkinson produced a key and unlocked it.

The cell was larger than Chavasse had anticipated. There were three small slit windows glazed with armour glass and in any case too small to admit a man. There was also a washbasin and a fixed toilet in one corner.

There was a single bed against each wall and Youngblood was lying on one of them reading a magazine. He looked at them in an almost casual fashion and didn't bother getting up.

"I've got a cell mate for you, Youngblood." Atkinson told him. "The governors afraid you might pass away on us one night without any warning. He'd like someone to be here just in case."

"Well, that's nice of the old bastard," Youngblood said. "I didn't know he cared."

"You just mind your bloody lip."

"Careful, Mr. Atkinson," Youngblood smiled. "There's a thin line of foam on the edge of your lips. You want to watch it."

Atkinson took one quick step towards him and Youngblood raised a hand. "I'm not a well man, remember."

"That's right, I was forgetting." Atkinson laughed gently, "You may be a big man in here, Youngblood, but from where I stand you look pretty damned small. I laugh myself sick every time I lock the door."

Something moved in Harry Youngblood's eyes and for a moment, the habitual mocking smile was erased and he looked capable of murder.

"That's better," Atkinson said. "That's much better," and he went outside, the door clanging behind him with a grim finality.

"Bastard!" Youngblood said and turned to examine Chavasse. "So you're Drummond? We've been expecting you for a week now."

"Word certainly gets around."

"That's the nick for you—we're all just one big happy family. You'll like it here—it's got everything. Central heating, air conditioning, television—all we needed was a bit of class and now we've got you."

"What's that supposed to mean?"

"Come off it—you were a Captain in the Engineers before they kicked you out. Sandhurst and all that. I read about it in the papers when you were up at the Bailey."

"I've read about you too."

Youngblood sat on the edge of the bed and lit a cigarette. "Where was that then?"

"A book called *Great Crimes of the Century*. Came out last year. There was a whole chapter devoted to the Peterfield Airport job. Written by a man called Tillotson."

"That clown," Youngblood said contemptuously. "He didn't get the half of it. Came to see me by special permission of the Home Office. I gave him all the griff—no reason not to now—but did he get it right? Gave all the credit for the planning to Ben Hoffa and *he* couldn't tell his arse from his elbow."

"It was your idea then?"

"That's it." Youngblood shrugged. "I needed Ben, I'm not denying that. He could fly a Dakota— that was his main function."

"What about Saxon?"

"A good lad when he had someone to tell him what to do."

"Any idea where they are now?"

"Somewhere in the sun spending all that lovely lolly if they've any sense."

"You never know your luck," Chavasse said. "They might be making arrangements for you to join them right now."

Youngblood stared across at him blankly. "Get me out you mean? Out of Fridaythorpe?" He exploded into laughter. "Have *you* got a lot to learn. No one gets out of here, didn't they tell you that? They've got television cameras and electronic gates—they've even constructed special walls of reinforced concrete with foundations twenty feet deep. That's just in case anyone ever thought of tunnelling." He shook his head. "This is it—the big cage—there *is* no way out."

"There's always a way," Chavasse said.

"What have we got here then? A Brain?"

"Big enough."

"It didn't do you much good on that Lonsdale Metals caper. You're here, aren't you?"

"So are you."

"Only because of Ben Hoffa and that bloody bird of his." For a moment Youngblood was genuinely angry. "He tried to drop her and she shopped him. That was the end for all of us."

"But they didn't get the money."

"That's it, boy." Youngblood grinned. "More than you can say."

"I know," Chavasse said feelingly. "I had the same trouble as Hoffa."

He sat there on the edge of the bed staring down at the floor as if momentarily depressed and Youngblood produced a twenty packet of cigarettes and offered him one. "Don't let it get you down. Between you and me that was quite something you pulled off. A pity you still had your amateur status. A bit more know-how and you might have got away with it."

"You seem to be doing all right for yourself," Chavasse said, holding up the cigarette.

Youngblood grinned and lolled back against the pillow. "I'm not complaining. I get as many of those things as I want and don't ask me how. When the blokes in here want snout they come to me and no one else. You fell on your feet when old man Carter decided to put you in here."

"He told me you'd been ill. How bad is it?"

"I had a slight stroke a month or two back. Nothing much." Youngblood shrugged. "Just one of those things."

"I got the impression he was afraid you might peg out on him one of these nights. If he's as worried as that why doesn't he have you transferred to the Scrubs?"

Youngblood chuckled harshly. "The Home Office would never wear that. They'd be frightened to death one of the London mobs might have a go at breaking me out in the hopes of getting their hot little hands on the lolly." He shook his head. "No, here I am and here I stay."

"For another fifteen years?"

Youngblood turned his head and smiled softly. "That remains to be seen, doesn't it?" He tossed the cigarettes across. "Have another."

He quite obviously wanted to talk and Chavasse lay there smoking and let him. He covered just about everything that had ever happened to him, starting with his years in a Camberwell orphanage and dwelling particularly on his time in the Navy. He wasn't married and apparently had only one living relative—a sister.

"You've got to look out for yourself, boy," he told Chavasse. "I learned that early. There's always some bastard waiting to take away what you've got. When I was a P.O. in MTBs I had a skipper called Johnson—young sub-lieutenant. Bloody

useless. I carried him—carried him. We took part in
the St. Laurent commando raid; he got hit early on.
He just sat there helpless in the skipper's chair on
the bridge bleeding to death. There was nothing we
could do for him. I took over, pressed home the
attack and put two torpedoes into an enemy
destroyer. And what happened when we got back?
Johnson got a posthumous Victoria Cross—I got a
bloody mention in dispatches."

*Funny how a story changed according to one's
point of view.* Chavasse stared up at the ceiling
remembering the official report of the action in the
file on Youngblood which had been compiled by S2
at the Bureau. The plain unvarnished truth was
that Johnson had signed his own death warrant by
staying in command on the bridge and undoubtedly aggravating his already serious injuries.
Youngblood had done well—and behaved steadily
under fire—there was no question about his personal courage, but at all times he had acted under
Johnson's direct orders.

He wondered now if Youngblood really believed
his own account of the action, but then he had probably told it to others and himself so many times
over the years that what might have been had
become reality. Somehow in the fantasy version
there was even an implication that the V.C. had
gone to the wrong person although he himself
would probably have indignantly denied the fact.

"According to Tillotson you were hit for smuggling first."

"That's right," Youngblood grinned. "Worked in
the Channel run in a converted MTB for a couple of
years following the war."

"What were you running—brandy?"

"Anything that would sell and almost anything would in those days. Booze, fags, nylons, watches."

"What about dope? I hear there's a lot of money in it."

"What in the hell do you think I am?" Youngblood demanded. "I wouldn't dirty my hands on that sort of rubbish."

It seemed a perfectly genuine reaction and was completely in character with the facts of his file. Harry Youngblood would never touch drugs or prostitution, two of the biggest money-spinners there were—a nice moral touch that. The newspapers had made a lot out of it at the time of his trial and the public had responded well, forgetting about the pilot of the Dakota hijacked at Peterfield who, in attempting to put up a fight, had been beaten so savagely by Youngblood that his eyesight was permanently affected.

And there were others. Over the years the police had pulled in Harry Youngblood again and again in connection with indictable offenses, mainly robbery which had too often included use of violence. At no time had they been able to make a charge stick and on one occasion, the night watchman of a fur warehouse, clubbed into insensibility, had afterwards died.

Chavasse surfaced and realised that Youngblood was still talking. "Those were the days, boy. We really gave the coppers a thing or two to think about. I had the beast team in the Smoke. One job after another and every one planned so well that the busies could never put a finger on us."

"That must have taken some doing."

"Oh, they pulled me in—every time there was a big tickle they tried to pin it on me. I spent half my time on the steps at West End Central being photographed. I was never out of the bloody papers."

"Until now."

Youngblood grinned. "You wait, boy—just wait. I'll be smiling right off the front page again at the bastards one of these days and there won't be a thing they can do about it."

Chavasse lay there on the bed thinking about the whole business. What was it Tillotson had said about Youngblood in his book? That he had a craving for notoriety that almost amounted to a death wish. Excitement and danger were meat and drink to him. He had enjoyed playing the gangster, being pulled in by the police time-after-time for questioning, having his picture in the papers.

One thing was certain. Here was no Robin Hood. This was a brutal and resourceful criminal whose easy smile concealed an iron will and a determination to have what he wanted whatever the cost.

Chavasse started to unlace his boots. "Think I'll turn in. It's been a long day."

Youngblood glanced over the top of the magazine. "You do that, boy." He grinned. "And don't let the bastards grind you down."

Chavasse hitched the blanket over his shoulder and closed his eyes. He wondered what it was going to be like in the machine shop. Car number plates Atkinson had said. Well, that was a damned sight better than sewing mail bags for a living. If only the screws were decent, life might be quite reasonable.

He frowned suddenly. So now he was even thinking like a con? A fine touch of irony there. Mallory would like that. Chavasse turned his face to the wall and slept.

4

Rough Justice

"Rehabilitation!" Youngblood shouted above the roar of the machine shop. "Marvellous, isn't it? Just think of all those clever bastards sitting in their private suites at the Home Office persuading themselves that just because they've given you the opportunity of learning a trade, you'll go out into the world a better and wiser man and lead a life of honest toil making car number plates for ten quid a week."

Chavasse positioned the plate he was holding carefully in the die stamping machine and pulled the lever. There was a slight hiss from the hydraulic press and he raised it to examine the number now etched firmly in pressed steel. He picked up a file and started to clean the rough edges of metal, thinking about what Youngblood had just said.

He was right, that was the damnable thing. After four weeks in the machine shop Chavasse had learned that lesson at least. He glanced across at Charlie Harker, a one-time chartered accountant doing seven years for embezzlement, and his machine partner, Rodgers, the mild-mannered little schoolmaster who was doing life for murdering his wife after finding her in bed with another man. How on earth did you rehabilitate such men by teaching them one of the lowest paid forms of semi-skilled work in industry?

Such thoughts were dangerous, but difficult to avoid. He had, after all, become one of these men— was in fact treated with some deference in a society where the scale of one's crime determined position in the social structure. As Paul Drummond serving six years for armed robbery and the theft of forty-five thousand pounds, Chavasse could easily have found himself on the top rung of the ladder had that not already been occupied by Harry Youngblood.

Rodgers came across and put another batch of blank plates on the bench. "All yours, Drum," he said and moved away.

He looked tired and there was sweat on his face so that his spectacles kept slipping down his nose and Chavasse was aware of a sudden sympathy. The man wasn't fit for this kind of work—why on earth couldn't the screws see that? But there was no time to consider individual needs here—life was cyclical, revolving around a time-table that must be observed at all costs.

But to hell with that. He wasn't here to do a survey for the Society for Prison Reform. He was here to watch Harry Youngblood—to worm his way into the man's confidence and to find out as much about him and his future plans as possible.

Strangely enough they had become good friends. Youngblood, like most great criminals, was a highly complex individual, flawed clean down the middle like a bell that looked fine until you tried to ring it.

Even his fellow prisoners had difficulty in understanding him. He had an ability to adapt to the company in which he found himself that was uncanny and the death wish was present in everything he did, the reckless reaching out to crash head on with danger which had probably contributed to his downfall more than any other single reason.

There was a story told of him that on one occasion when casing a Mayfair mansion prior to a robbery, he had attended a soirée there uninvited, charming everyone in sight and leaving with the purse from his hostess's handbag. Stopped by a down-and-out with a hard luck story on the pavement outside, Youngblood had presented him with the twenty-five pounds the purse had contained and had gone on his way cheerfully.

Kind and considerate, he could be generous to a fault as Chavasse had already discovered, especially when there was no danger of any personal inconvenience. He could also be hard, brutal and utterly ruthless when crossed and in the final analysis, was only interested in his own well being.

He grinned across at Chavasse. "Cheer up, Drum. It may never happen."

Chavasse smiled back, avoiding a frown by only a fraction of a second. Youngblood was normally good-humoured, but for the past two days he had positively overflowed which must indicate something.

His train of thought was interrupted by the arrival of a convict called Brady pushing a trolley loaded with finished plates.

"Anything for me?" he demanded.

Chavasse nodded brusquely at the pile on the end of the bench. He didn't care for Brady who was serving ten years for housebreaking which had also involved the rape of a woman of sixty-five. He had the sort of face that went with the average citizen's conception of a thieves' kitchen and his voice was roughened by years of disease and liquor.

"How about some snout, Harry?" he asked Youngblood as he started to load the trolley.

"You owe me for three weeks already," Youngblood said. "No more till you've paid something on account."

"Have a heart, Harry?" Brady grabbed his arm. "I haven't had a fag for two days. I'm going crazy."

"Don't kid yourself," Youngblood said coldy. "You're already there; they should have had you in for treatment years ago. Now clear off. You're bothering me."

With a man like Brady it didn't take much. Chavasse had moved to the end of the bench to get some rivets and as he turned, caught sight of Brady's face contorted with uncontrollable rage. He snatched up a rat's tail file, the end pointed, sharp as any stiletto and swung it above his head, ready to plunge it down into Youngblood's unprotected back.

There was no time for any warning and Chavasse snatched up a hammer and threw it with all his force. It caught Brady in the chest and he cried out in pain and dropped the file as he staggered back.

Youngblood swung around, taking in the file and the hammer, the expression on Brady's face and when he turned and glanced at Chavasse his eyes were like pieces of black stone.

He picked up the file and held it out. "This yours, Jack?"

Brady stood there staring at him, sweat on his face. Quite suddenly he grabbed the trolley and pushed it away hurriedly.

Work had not flagged, the noise had remained at the same level and yet there wasn't a man at that end of the room who had failed to note the incident and Chavasse was aware of two things. Youngblood's slight nod to Nevinson, a tall heavily built Scot on the other side of the room, and the approach of Meadows, one of the screws.

"What's going on here?" he demanded.

"Not a thing, Mr. Meadows, sir," Youngblood said. "We're all working like the clappers."

Meadows was young and not long out of the army, the dark smudge of moustache on his upper lip an indication of his desperate attempt to always appear older than he was. He turned to Chavasse who stood at the end of the bench, hands at his sides. Meadows had never risen above the rank of lance corporal and ex-captains fallen on hard times were meat and drink to him.

"And what the devil do you think you're supposed to be doing, Drummond?" he demanded. "I know the idea of soiling those lily-white hands of yours doesn't appeal, but work *is* the object of the exercise."

Youngblood moved in very close and said softly, "He is working, Mr. Meadows, sir. He's working very hard. Now why don't you go back to the other end of the room like a good little boy."

And Meadows took it, that was the important thing. His hesitation was only momentary, his face quite white and he was afraid, which was all that mattered.

From the other end of the room there came a sudden cry of agony. Meadows turned, glad of the excuse and hurried away. Everyone stopped working, all noise dying as the machines were switched off one-by-one. Nevinson appeared, walking close to the wall, wiping his hands on an oily rag.

"What happened, Jock?" Youngblood called.

"Jack Brady's just had a nasty accident," Nevinson said calmly. "Spilt a bucket of boiling water over his legs in the blacksmith's shop."

Youngblood shook his head as he glanced at Chavasse. "Now that was careless of him, wasn't it?"

Chavasse said nothing and moved forward with the others. Brady was groaning in agony and kept it up till the first aid men arrived and one of them gave him an injection. He lay there writhing, his great, ugly face soaked in sweat as they got him on to a stretcher. He moaned again and lost consciousness as they lifted him up, but it was difficult to feel any sort of compassion for him. He had broken the code of the society in which he lived and had received in return justice of a sort.

More screws had arrived, Atkinson among them and he rapped his staff on a bench. "Get back to work, all of you." He turned to Meadows. "I'll want a report on my desk in an hour, Mr. Meadows. I'll send someone to relieve you." He walked to the door and paused. "You can bring Drummond with you when you come—his sister's here to see him."

*   *   *

The last Thursday in every month was a general visiting day and when the Duty Officer took Chavasse into the main hall, it was already pretty full. A row of cubicles stretched from one wall to the other, and in each one prisoner and visitor faced each other through a sheet of armoured glass and spoke through microphones.

They sat Chavasse in a cubicle and he waited impatiently, the voices on either side a meaningless blur and then the door opposite opened and Jean Frazer came in. She was wearing a white nylon blouse and a neat two piece suit in Donegal tweed with a pleated skirt. Strange, but he had never realised before just how attractive she really was.

Her ready smile faded as she sank down into the chair opposite. "Paul, what have they done to you?"

Her voice sounded slightly distorted over the amplifier and he smiled. "Do I look that bad?"

"I wouldn't have believed it possible."

He cracked suddenly, a savage, cutting edge to his voice. "For God's sake, Jean, what do you think it's like in here? I'm not Paul Chavasse playing a part and going home nights. I'm Paul Drummond doing six years for armed robbery. I've been inside four months now. I think like a con, I act like one. Most important of all, I'm treated like one—tell Graham Mallory to stuff that in his blasted pipe."

There was real pain in her eyes and she reached out to touch him, forgetting about the glass. "I feel so damned inadequate."

He grinned. "A good thing there's glass between

us. You look good enough to eat, never mind the other thing."

She managed to smile. "Do I?"

"Now don't go making any rash promises. They'd only get you into trouble. After all, I do anticipate getting out of here sometime. How *is* Mallory, by the way?"

"His usual charming self. He told me to tell you to get a move on. Apparently he could use you elsewhere and thinks this business has gone on long enough."

"The answer I'd like to send him is completely unprintable," Chavasse said. "But never mind. We'd better get down to business. We're only allowed ten minutes."

"How are you and Youngblood getting on?"

"Fine—in fact I managed to stop someone sticking a sharp implement into him this morning."

"I thought they put people in prison to prevent them doing that sort of thing?"

"That's the theory—worked out by people who don't know what they're talking about as usual."

"Have you found anything out about the Baron?"

He shook his head. "I've heard his name mentioned in general gossip amongst the other prisoners, but he's as much a question mark to them as he is to me. I tried to talk about him with Youngblood—told him I'd heard the Baron had got Saxton and Hoffa out. He seemed to think the whole idea was fairy tales for the kiddies."

"So you've really wasted your time?"

"Not on your life. Youngblood's on his way out of

here. I've never been so certain of anything in my life. He hasn't said so in so many words, but everything about him confirms it. His general manner, the remarks he makes and so on."

"You've no idea how or when?"

He shook his head. "Not a clue. There is one thing. He seems to be feeling his oats a bit at the moment. I think something's in the air."

She shook her head. "It doesn't make sense, Paul. I've read the file on this place. He couldn't get out—nobody could."

"He's going to go, there's nothing surer and I'd like to be there when he does."

"You'll stop him, of course."

"Not on your life, angel," Chavasse grinned. "He doesn't know it yet, but I'm going with him."

There was immediate dismay in her eyes, but as she opened her mouth to reply, a prison officer approached. "Time's up, miss."

She got to her feet. "Goodbye, Paul. Look after yourself."

"You, too," he said and turned and followed the Duty Officer out.

Meals at Fridaythorpe were taken in a small canteen on the second floor of each tower block and when Chavasse arrived, lunch had already started.

The officer in charge signed for him and he went down to the counter and filled a tray quickly. Youngblood was sitting at the first table near the wall and he waved, pointing to a vacant place next to him.

"A sister, eh?" he commented as Chavasse sat down. "You've been holding out on me."

"I wasn't sure she'd want to know me any more," Chavasse said. "I must take a lot of living up to."

"I hear she looked pretty good."

Chavasse had long since got over being surprised at Youngblood's apparently inexhaustible supply of information. "Is there anything you don't hear?"

"If there is, it isn't worth knowing."

Atkinson arrived on one of his periodical tours of inspection and a few minutes later, the bell rang for the end of the session. They queued to return their plates and then stood in line at the lift to be returned in batches to their cells for the rest period before the afternoon session in the workshops began.

Smoking was allowed as they waited and Youngblood produced a cigarette, put it in his mouth and searched unsuccessfully for a match. Atkinson stopped beside him, took a box from his pocket and held it out.

"You can keep those, Youngblood, but make 'em last." He shook his head as he moved away. "I don't know what some of you blokes would do without me."

There was a certain amount of dutiful laughter, particularly from those who wanted to stay in his good books. A moment later, the lift arrived and as they moved forward, Youngblood put his cigarette away and slipped the matches into his pocket.

Chavasse was conscious of a sudden surge of excitement. The whole incident was completely out of character. There was no love lost between Atkinson and Youngblood, both men made that quite plain, and yet the Principal Officer had gone out of his way to do Youngblood a kindness. It just didn't make sense.

During the rest period the cell doors were left open and there was a certain amount of coming and going, but any prisoner was at liberty to lock himself in if he didn't feel sociable.

"You don't mind if I close the door, do you?" Youngblood said to Chavasse when they reached their cell. "I'm not in the mood for fraternising today."

"Suits me." Chavasse stretched out on his bed. "What's wrong—aren't you feeling so good?"

"Restless," Youngblood said. "Let's say I feel like cracking the walls wide open and leave it at that."

Chavasse opened a magazine and waited and after a while Youngblood got to his feet and moved to the washbasin. He lit a cigarette, keeping his back turned and then placed the box of matches on the side of the basin.

Chavasse took a cigarette from one of his shirt pockets, got to his feet and moved forward quickly, reaching for the matches. Youngblood was staring down at his open palm. He closed it quickly, but not before Chavasse had seen the small brown capsule.

"Mind if I have a match, Harry?"

"Help yourself," Youngblood said.

Chavasse lit the cigarette and returned to his bed. *So Atkinson was the contact man?* They must have paid him a small fortune, but then, there was a lot at stake. He lay down and behind him, Youngblood filled a plastic cup with water and drank it slowly.

There was a strange fixed expression on his face as he sat on the edge of his bed and Chavasse said,

"You sure you're okay, Harry? You don't look too good to me. Maybe you should go sick."

"I'm fine," Youngblood said. "Just fine. Probably the spring and all that jazz. I always get restless at this time of year. It's the gypsy in me."

"Who wouldn't in a dump like this," Chavasse said, but Youngblood didn't seem to hear him and sat there staring at the wall, a strange far-away look in his eyes.

It was hotter than usual in the machine shop that afternoon, mainly because the air circulating system had broken down, and most of the men had stripped to the waist.

Chavasse worked at one end of the bench cutting plates with a hand guillotine and Youngblood was grinding steel clips to size on a high speed wheel. He had been sweating profusely for some time now and there was a strange dazed expression in his eyes.

"You all right, Harry?" Chavasse called, but Youngblood didn't seem to hear him.

He paused for a moment, leaning heavily on the bench, rubbing sweat away from his eyes and when he reached out to pick up another clip from the stack on the bench beside him his hand was trembling. He groped ineffectually for a moment and then the whole pile went over, one of the clips ricocheted from the wheel like a bullet in a shower of sparks.

And then Youngblood started to shake. He staggered back, rebounding from the bench behind, driving headfirst into the mass of working machinery opposite.

Chavasse got to him just in time. Youngblood's eyes had retracted, sweat poured from his body and his limbs jerked convulsively. There was no question, but that he was undergoing a perfectly genuine fit, however it had been induced—the second stroke for which the governor had been waiting, the one which would earn him a fast trip in an ambulance to Manningham General Hospital. And afterwards . . .?

There were cries of alarm from all parts of the workshop, a rush of feet and as Youngblood's body was racked by another convulsive spasm, Chavasse did the only possible thing and allowed himself to fall backwards across the bench still holding him. When he ran his left forearm along the edge of the grinder, the flesh split open in a nine-inch streak and blood spurted across the bench in a satisfying stream.

He started to slide to the ground, clutching at his arm, letting Youngblood fall and Nevinson caught him just in time. Strangely enough there was no pain and Chavasse sat there pressing his thumb in to the brachial artery in an attempt to stop the bright flow.

For a while there was considerable confusion and then Atkinson arrived, pushing his way through the crowd.

"What in the hell happened here?" he demanded of the Duty Officer.

"Youngblood threw another fit. He'd have gone into the machinery if Drummond hadn't caught him. He opened up his arm on the grinding wheel."

Atkinson inspected it briefly. "Doesn't look too good, does it?" He turned to the Duty Officer. "I want a couple of stretchers up here fast from sick bay and tell them to ring through to Manningham General. Tell them Youngblood's had another stroke and we're on our way."

"What about Drummond?"

"Him too, of course. You don't think we can deal with an injury like that here, do you? He's going to need a dozen stitches in that arm. Now get moving."

Strangely enough it was at that precise moment that Chavasse's arm started to hurt like hell.

5

Nightwatch

When he opened his eyes the room was festooned with cobwebs—giant grey cobwebs that stretched from one wall to the other and undulated slowly. He closed his eyes, fighting the panic that rose inside him. When he opened them again the cobwebs had almost disappeared.

He was lying in a narrow hospital bed and his left arm felt strangely numb. When he looked down he saw that it was heavily bandaged and then he remembered and looked around him.

The ward was small—no more than half a dozen beds. Two of them were occupied. One by Brady who lay with a cage over his legs, the other by Youngblood. Both men seemed to be either sleeping or unconscious.

Two prison officers were sitting at a small table by the door playing cards. As Chavasse stirred, they glanced across and one of them got to his feet and walked over.

"How do you feel?"

"Terrible." Chavasse tried to moisten dry lips. "What happened?"

"They gave you an anaesthetic and stitched you up." He turned to his companion. "Better get the doctor. He said he wanted to know when he came round."

Chavasse closed his eyes as the other officer picked up the telephone. His mouth was bone dry and he felt curiously light-headed, but otherwise he was fine. He looked down at the arm. He could feel nothing except that curious numbness which indicated the use of painkilling shots and he wondered how bad it was.

He'd taken one hell of a chance back there at the machine shop. What if he'd severed a tendon, for instance? He closed his eyes, sweat springing to his forehead, and opened them again in time to see one of the prison officers unlock the door.

The doctor who came in was African, a tall cheerful Nigerian with tribal caste marks prominent on one cheek and a ready smile. He sat on the edge of the bed and took Chavasse's pulse.

"How are you feeling?"

"A bit light-headed and my mouth's very dry."

"After-effects of the anaesthetic, that's all. Nothing to worry about." The Nigerian poured water into a glass from a jug on the bedside locker. "Drink this—you'll feel a lot better."

Chavasse did as he was told and then lay back. "What about my arm—is it serious?"

The Nigerian shook his head and grinned. "You'll play the violin again, isn't that what they would say on television? Thirteen stitches—I hope you are not superstitious, but I couldn't find room for an extra one."

"Are you sending me straight back?"

"To Fridaythorpe?" There was something close to compassion in the Nigerian's eyes when he replied. "No, I think we'll hang on to you for a day or two."

Chavasse tried hard not to show his relief, but in his weakened state found it impossible. "What about Youngblood—is he very illl?"

The Nigerian shrugged. "A second stroke is never a good thing. We'll know more after our tests tomorrow. But we've talked long enough. Now you must sleep again."

He went out and they locked the door behind him. The two screws went back to their card game and Chavasse turned and looked at Youngblood. He was sleeping peacefully, his face in repose looking strangely innocent. Chavasse took a deep breath. So—the stage was set? He wondered what the next act would be and still wondering, drifted into sleep.

When he next awakened it was night and the ward was a place of shadows, rain drumming against the windows. One of the prison officers slept soundly on an unoccupied bed, the other read a magazine at the table.

He glanced across as Chavasse stirred. "Are you all right?"

Chavasse nodded. "I think I'll take a walk."

He swung his legs to the floor, sat there for a moment and then got to his feet and walked to the washroom at the other end of the ward. It could have been worse—much worse and on the way back he felt even better.

When he sat down again on the edge of his bed he realised, with something of a shock, that Youngblood's eyes were wide open. He stared at Chavasse strangely, a slight frown on his face and Chavasse pulled a chair forward and sat down beside him.

"How are you feeling, Harry?"

"What is this?" Youngblood said. "What's going on?"

"You're in the closed ward at Manningham General. You had another stroke."

"What are you doing here?"

"When you blew your top at Fridaythorpe you almost went headfirst into the machinery. I caught you just in time. Opened up my arm on the grinding wheel in the process."

"Is it bad?"

"Thirteen stitches—could be worse. They're keeping me here for a couple of days."

The prison officer at the table make a quick phone call and then came over. "I've sent for the doctor. How do you feel?"

"Hungry as hell," Youngblood said. "Any chance of a meal?"

"We'll see what he says."

A moment later there was a knock at the door and he opened it to admit the Nigerian. He crossed to Youngblood's bed, sat down and made a quick examination. "Good—very good. You feel better for your sleep."

"What he really needs is something to eat," Chavasse said. "And so do I. We're both starving."

The Nigerian smiled. "I'll see what I can do, but

you must get back into bed." He turned to the prison officer. "I'll tell the kitchen to send something up, Mr. Carter. I'm going off duty now, but my colleague, Dr. Mackenzie, will be taking over. If you need anything, ring through to night sister, but in any case, he'll be looking in later on."

Carter locked the door behind him and returned to the bed. He was a middle-aged, rather kindly man who was thought by most of his colleagues to be too soft.

"Anything I can do for you?"

"I could manage a visit to the washroom," Youngblood said. "I never could stand these damned bedpans. Maybe you and Drummond could give me a hand."

They took him between them, Chavasse on the left so that he could use his good arm. He walked very slowly like an old man and they had to support almost his whole weight. Chavasse was sure he was bluffing, yet on the way back there was sweat on his forehead and when they got him on to the bed again, he seemed exhausted. On the other hand, that might be the after-effects of the drug . . .?

There was a knock on the door and when Carter opened it, a male nurse came in pushing a trolley. He served them with scrambled eggs, toast and tea, and went out again.

Chavasse took his time over the meal, watching Youngblood intently. He showed little desire for conversation and ate slowly, apparently still weak and yet there was a slight air of tension about him and he kept glancing at the electric clock on the wall.

When they had both finished, Carter took the

trays and put them back on the trolley which the nurse had left by the door.

"What about a smoke, Mr. Carter?" Youngblood said.

Carter looked dubious. "I'm not sure that's such a good idea."

"Just one—that's hardly likely to kill us."

"I suppose not."

He gave them a cigarette each and a light and went back to his magazine. It was just five minutes to nine and to Chavasse the atmosphere seemed to crackle with electricity. Youngblood lay back against the pillow, staring up at the ceiling, the cigarette held loosely between the fingers of his left hand—a hand that shook slightly each time he raised it to his mouth, betraying his inner tension.

As the second hand swept round towards nine he crushed his cigarette into the ashtray on the bedside locker and looked across at Chavasse.

"I'd like to say thanks while I still have the chance for what you did up there in the machine shop. First Brady and then the other thing."

"That's okay."

"I wish there was something I could do for you—I don't like being in debt to anyone—but there isn't. Whatever happens, I want you to get that straight."

"What in the hell are you talking about?"

Before Youngblood could reply, there was a knock on the door. Carter opened it on the chain and Chavasse heard a pleasant cultured voice, "Dr. Mackenzie—just making my rounds."

The man who stepped into the room wore the conventional white coat of the staff doctor and a stethoscope dangled from one pocket like a badge of office. He had a pale, aristocratic face and a fixed smile.

To the average person he might have seemed a slightly effeminate rather upper-class young man, but not to Chavasse who knew a real pro when he saw one.

"How are things then?" he said pleasantly and as Carter turned to lock the door, took a .38 automatic from one pocket and delivered a stunning blow to the base of the prison officer's skull.

Carter groaned and fell heavily to the floor. There was a cry of anger and the second prison officer, who had been sleeping on one of the spare beds, flung himself forward and landed squarely on Mackenzie's back before he could turn. He lurched into the wall, the gun flying from his hand to skid across the polished floor.

They went down together, Mackenzie underneath and then Youngblood arrived on the run. He grabbed the prison officer by the collar and pulled him off with a tremendous heave, swinging the man round, driving his clenched fist into his stomach. The prison officer doubled over and Youngblood's knee lifted him back against the wall. He slid to the ground and Mackenzie moved in fast and kicked him expertly in the side of the head.

"Almost fouled things up for us didn't he, old man?" he said to Youngblood as they stood over the two prison officers breathing heavily.

"A remarkable recovery, Harry," Chavasse said. "I must say you put in quite a performance back there in the machine shop."

He was standing three or four yards away, one hand behind his back as Youngblood turned to face him. "That was genuine enough, thanks to a drug called Mabofine. All the symptoms, but none of the after-effects."

"It must have taken quite some planning."

"A fascinating exchange," Mackenzie interrupted, "but I'm sure you won't mind if we postpone it and get to hell out of here."

"That suits me just fine," Chavasse said.

Mackenzie smiled patiently. "I'm afraid you'll have to sit this one out, old man. We've only catered for one."

"That's right, Drum," Youngblood said. "Fare paying passengers only this trip."

Chavasse took his hand from behind his back and held up Mackenzie's automatic. "This tells a different tale. It says we all go or nobody does."

Mackenzie's habitual slight smile disappeared and he slid one foot forward tentatively. "I wouldn't," Youngblood said heavily. "He means it."

Mackenzie shrugged. "The Baron isn't going to like this."

"To hell with the Baron. He can put it on the bill, can't he? Now how do we get out of here?"

"Suit yourself." Mackenzie opened the door and pulled in a wheelchair which had been standing outside. "A nice authentic touch just in case we meet anyone. We take the service elevator at the end of the corridor to the basement and go out through the staff entrance. There's no one about at this time of night. I've got transport waiting and clothes for one." He turned to Chavasse. "I don't know how far you think you'll get in hospital pyjamas and a dressing gown."

"No problem there." Chavasse gestured toward Carter. "He's about my size. Get him stripped. I'll manage just fine with his trousers and shirt and that pullover he's wearing under his uniform jacket."

They didn't argue and a few moments later Youngblood tossed the clothes across, Chavasse withdrew to the end of the ward, placed the gun within easy reach and dressed quickly.

"It isn't that I don't trust you, Harry," he explained. "It's just that I know you'd cut my throat if you thought there was even a remote possibility that I might spoil your chances."

Youngblood chuckled and shook his head in frank admiration. "A pity we didn't meet up years ago, Drum. We could have taken them all on."

He sat in the wheelchair, arranging a blanket over his legs and Mackenzie took off his white coat and threw it at Chavasse. "You wear that and push the wheelchair—I'll swing the stethoscope in one hand."

"Aren't we gong to tie these two up?"

"Not worth it. The real Mackenzie could turn up at any time. Now let's get moving. We've got a tight schedule."

It was quiet in the corridor and when Mackenzie pressed the button, the lift rose to meet them at once. When the doors opened in the basement he walked out without hesitation and Chavasse followed him pushing the wheelchair.

The basement was deserted except for two ambulances parked by a loading bay and they kept on going through the staff door at the end and out into the night.

Rain drifted in a fine spray through the light over the porch. An old Commer van was parked at the bottom of the steps and Mackenzie peered out cautiously. Two nurses, uniform caps swinging from their shoulders against the rain, were walking down towards the main gates, but otherwise the drive was deserted.

Mackenzie went down the steps, opened the rear door of the van, turned and nodded. Chavasse and Youngblood went after him. The door slammed, a key turned and they were driven rapidly away.

A few moments after starting, an interior light came on and Youngblood discovered a pile of clothing in one corner. There was everything he needed from shoes to a raincoat, all obviously carefully chosen for size.

The van was not being driven at any particular speed and he had little difficulty in changing. He had barely finished when they braked to a halt. The engine was switched off, Mackenzie jumped out, came round to the rear and unlocked the door.

"Let's be having you."

They were in a large town-centre car park and buildings lifted into the night on either side. "Where are we?" Youngblood demanded. "Manningham?"

"A change of transport, that's all." Mackenzie handed Chavasse a Burberry trenchcoat and a silk scarf. "Much as I regret having to part with them you'd better have these. Do you think I could possibly have my gun back now?"

"A fair exchange." Chavasse handed him the automatic and pulled on the raincoat.

Mackenzie withdrew the magazine then snapped it back into place with an ominous click. "I'm awfully tempted, old man. I really am."

"I'm sure you are," Chavasse said. "On the other hand it would make a hell of a dent in your plans to have me lying around in a ditch somewhere. Now that really would have every copper in the country straining at the leash."

"Somehow that's what I thought you might say," Mackenzie said. "Another time perhaps. Shall we go?"

The car waited in the shadows of the far side of the park, a Vauxhall brake, and Mackenzie drove away at once, taking a road which had them out of Manningham and into the countryside within ten minutes.

He switched on the radio and as music drifted out, leaned back in the driving seat, his eyes on the road. "And now we can get down to business, Mr. Youngblood."

"I was wondering when you'd get round to it."

Mackenzie laughed gently. "Do you know something? That's exactly what Ben Hoffa said."

Youngblood turned to look at him. "You handled Ben's break?"

"But of course. The Baron always gives me the big ones."

"Where is he now?"

"Hoffa?" Mackenzie chuckled. "A long, long way away, Mr. Youngblood. I can assure you of that and they won't get him back. That's all part of our guaranteed service. But let's dispose of the sordid cash angle first. You know our terms—they were fully explained. We've kept our part of the bargain—

we've got you out. You tell us where the cash is and that completes Phase One of the operation."

"There *is* no cash," Youngblood said calmly.

The car swerved and Mackenzie fought to regain control. "You're joking of course."

"Not at all. I did a deal with some Dutch money changers in Amsterdam and converted my share into diamonds—two hundred and fifty thousand pounds' worth."

"Not bad—not bad at all. Prices have risen a lot in five years. Where are they?"

"A safe deposit in Jermyn Street in London in the name of Alfred Bonner. One of those places where the manager keeps one key and the customer the other. You need both to open the box."

"And who has yours?"

"My sister. She lives at 15 Wheeler Court, Bethnal Green. She'll hand it over with no trouble. I put her in the picture when she last visited me three months ago."

"That all sounds perfectly straightforward," Mackenzie said. "I'll pass the information along to the right quarter."

"And what happens to us?"

"You'll be well taken care of. If everything goes according to plan, they'll start Phase Two when the Baron has his hands on those diamonds. I should point out, by the way, that Mr. Drummond here is very definitely going to come extra."

"And when do we get to see the Baron?" Chavasse said.

"When he's ready and not before. Under our system you're passed on from hand to hand as it were. We find that much safer for all concerned."

"With the Baron waiting at the end with my money, I hope?" Youngblood said.

"Plus a new identity, a new life, a passport to anywhere in the world. I should have thought that was quite a bargain, old man."

Ahead was an intersection and he turned left into a quiet secondary road and braked to a halt about a mile further on. It had stopped raining and a full moon had appeared from behind a bank of heavy cloud so that they could see quite clearly a five barred gate and a ruined farmhouse beyond.

"All out!" Mackenzie said. "This is where I leave you."

Youngblood and Chavasse stepped on to the grass verge and looked around them. "What is this?" Youngblood demanded.

Mackenzie slipped off his watch and gave it to him through the window. "It's now nine thirty-five. In approximately ten minutes someone will pick you up."

"What's he driving?" Chavasse asked.

"I've no idea. His opening words will be: Is there anywhere in particular you'd like me to take you? You must answer: Babylon. He'll tell you Babylon's too far for him, but will offer to take you part of the way. Have you got that?"

Youngblood stared at him in amazement. "Are you crazy?"

"If I am, then you've made a damned bad bargain, old man," Mackenzie said and he released the handbrake and drove rapidly away.

They stood there, listening to the engine fade into the distance and when it had finally died Youngblood turned to Chavasse, face white in the moonlight.

"What do you think? Are they just stringing us along?"

"I shouldn't have thought so. They've too much to lose."

"I suppose you're right. Better have a cigarette and hope for the best."

It was Chavasse who heard the sound of the approaching vehicle first and he moved out into the road and looked down to the shadows at the bottom of the hill where headlights flared through the darkness.

"Could this be it?" Youngblood demanded.

Chavasse watched for a moment, eyes narrowed and then shook his head. "I shouldn't imagine so. It looks like a petrol tanker to me."

6

In a Lonely Place

The man who had impersonated Mackenzie turned on to the Great North Road, pulled up at the first roadside cafe he came to and went into a phone box. He made two calls and the first took some getting as it was apparently routed through a manual exchange. It was at least five minutes before a blunt Yorkshire voice sounded on the other end of the line and he cut in at once.

"That you, Mr. Crowther. Look, we've run into a little difficulty. That package you've been expecting—you'll actually be receiving two. Think you can handle them? We'll double your fee naturally."

Crowther might have been discussing the price of cattle and his voice was completely matter-of-fact when he replied. "I don't see why not. It might take a bit longer, that's all. We'll have to go careful. Another thing, my wife died yesterday."

"Sorry to hear that."

"We're burying her in the morning and that won't help. Still, leave it with me. I'm sure we'll manage."

"I'll be in touch."

He replaced the receiver and found some more change. This time he dialled a London number. The receiver was lifted at once at the other end and a woman said, "World Wide Exports."

"Hello, sweetie—Simon Vaughan speaking from dear old County Durham."

"What happened? I've just been watching the news on television. It seems two birds have flown the coop, not one."

"Couldn't be helped, I'm afraid. I'm not too happy about the additional package. Something about him seems wildly wrong to me. Still, it doesn't matter. Crowther's agreed to take on both of them—for twice his usual fee."

"I'll pass the word along. What about the merchandise?"

"It's in a safe deposit in Jermyn Street under the name of Alfred Bonner. Not what we expected, by the way, but something equally as good."

"What about a key?"

"The sister has it at 15, Wheeler Court, Bethnal Green. There shouldn't be any hitch there. She's expecting a caller."

"Good—we'll pick it up right away. And Simon. . . ."

"Yes, sweetie?"

"I'd check on Crowther tomorrow if I were you."

"Exactly what I was thinking, I'll see you in church."

As he walked back to his car, he whistled softly and there was a smile on his face.

When Chavasse climbed out of the tanker's secret

compartment it had stopped raining and he waited for Youngblood to join him, shivering slightly in the chill wind. The driver dropped the hatch back into place and looked down at them.

"There's a track on the other side of the road. You'll be met. Good luck."

He climbed back inside the cab, there was a hiss of air as he released the brakes and the tanker faded into the night.

Chavasse watched the red tail lights dwindle away and turned to Youngblood. "What time is it?"

"Just coming up to half one."

"Which means we were inside that sardine can for almost four hours. I reckon we must have covered the best part of a hundred and fifty miles."

"I know one thing," Youngblood said with feeling. "It was never intended to hold two."

Somewhere in the distance a dog barked hollowly and then a bank of cloud rolled away from the moon and the countryside was bathed in a hard white light. The night sky was incredibly beautiful with stars strung away to the horizon and hills lifted uneasily into the darkness all round.

"Where in the hell are we?" Youngblood demanded.

On the other side of the road, a stone rattled and a young woman moved out of the shadows. "Is there anywhere in particular you'd like me to take you?"

Chavasse recognised her accent at once and turned to Youngblood. "Some part of Yorkshire, that's certain."

The girl wore a headscarf and an old raincoat and waited patiently, her face calm, touched with an impossible beauty by the hard white light of the moon.

"Babylon," Youngblood said.

"Too far for me, but I can take you part of the way," she said in her strange, dead voice.

She moved back up the track and Youngblood turned to Chavasse in exasperation. "This whole bloody affair is getting more like something out of *Alice in Wonderland* every minute. We'll be meeting the White Rabbit next."

"Or the Mad Hatter," Chavasse said with a grin and went after the girl quickly.

Sam Crowther watched them coming along the track clear in the moonlight from the loft of his barn. "Here they are," he said softly.

There was a stirring in the darkness at his side and Billy leaned forward excitedly, saliva dribbling from the corner of his mouth.

"Two nuts to crack this time, Billy," Crowther said. "But we'll manage, won't we? All in good time."

He patted Billy on the shoulder and went down the ladder. As he emerged from the barn, the girl turned in through the gate, Chavasse and Youngblood followed her.

"Good lass, Molly," Crowther said. "You go in and make 'em some ham and eggs."

The girl moved off without a word and Crowther turned with a big smile, holding out his hand. "Mr. Youngblood and Mr. Drummond, I presume. There was so much about you two on the eleven o'clock news that I feel I've known you all my life. I'm Sam Crowther."

Youngblood ignored the hand. "And what's that?" He nodded to Billy who had just shambled out of the shadows of the barn.

"Only Billy, Mr. Youngblood. Only Billy." Crowther chuckled and tapped his forehead significantly. "He's not got all he needs upstairs, but he's as good as two ordinary men round the farm. But what are we standing round here for? You come on in and I'll show you your room. By the time you've washed up Molly will have a meal on the table, I've no doubt."

"Your daughter?" Chavasse said as they went into the porch.

"That's it, Mr. Drummond. A good girl, our Molly."

"She doesn't seem to have much to say for herself."

"Not so surprising," Crowther said piously. "And her mother barely twenty-four hours cold." There was a door to the left and he opened it to disclose a cheap deal coffin with gilt handles standing on a table. "We're putting her under at the village church at ten o'clock in the morning. It's eight miles away so that means the hearse will be here at nine. You gentlemen will have to lay low till it's gone."

He closed the door and led the way up a flight of narrow wooden stairs covered in cheap linoleum worn smooth by the years. The landing was long and narrow and he opened the door at the far end and switched on the light.

"I think you'll be comfortable enough here."

There was an old double bed with a brass frame,

a wardrobe and dressing table in Victorian mahogany and a marble washstand.

Youngblood unbuttoned his raincoat and threw it on the bed. "And how long do we stay here?"

"Until I get the right telephone call. Could be tomorrow. The day after at the latest. But don't worry. You're safe enough here. We're miles from anywhere."

"And where exactly would that be?" Chavasse asked.

Crowther gave him a sly grin. "That would be telling, now wouldn't it, Mr. Drummond? No, I couldn't do that. I've got myself to protect. You gents come down when you're ready. There'll be food on the table."

The door closed behind him and Youngblood took off his jacket and draped it over a chair. "What do you think?"

"I wouldn't trust him out of my sight for very long." Chavasse moved to the window and peered outside. "This place is like a bad film set for *Wuthering Heights*."

Youngblood poured water from a large jug into a cracked basin and swilled his face and neck. "I know one thing," he said as he towelled himself briskly. "He only has to make one wrong move and I'll break his bloody neck."

Chavasse took off his raincoat and moved across to the basin. "I've a feeling that might not be so easy where our boy Billy's concerned."

"You've got a point there, but why cross bridges?" Youngblood grinned. "Right now I'm more interested in ham and eggs. I'll see you downstairs."

The door closed softly behind him and Chavasse
stood frowning into the cracked mirror above the
washstand. There was something wrong here, he
had never been more certain of anything in his life.
It spoke aloud in the girl's silence, in the slyness in
Crowther's eyes when he glanced sideways, in the
great shambling imbecile that was his shadow. But
if something sinister was intended, what could
it be? Crowther was no fool, that was obvious and
must realise that together, Chavasse and Youngblood presented a formidable combination. Sepa-
rated on the other hand . . . With a sudden
exclamation, he hurled the towel from him,
wrenched open the door and hurried downstairs.

When Youngblood went into the parlour there
was no one there and he moved along the passage
and entered the kitchen. Molly was standing at the
stove in an old cotton dress that was a size too small
so that the skirt seams had split in several places.
She wore no stockings and when she turned to look
at him he realised, with considerable disappoint-
ment, that the moon had lied. She was at best plain
and with her high cheekbones, olive skin and over-
full lips, many people would have considered her
ugly.

"It's almost ready," she said in that strange,
dead voice of hers and smoothed her hands over her
thighs. "I'm just going out to the shed to get some
more wood for the stove."

She took a lantern down from a hook above the
sink, lit it and moved towards the back door.
Youngblood was there before her. "Here, I'll take

that," he said. "You could probably do with some help."

She hesitated, gazing up at him, a strange uncertain expression in her eyes and then she handed him the lamp. "All right. It's across the yard."

The cobbles were damp in the night air and treacherous underfoot and Youngblood picked his way carefully, cursing when he stepped into a puddle and water slopped into one of his shoes. When the girl opened the door of the shed, he could smell mouldy hay, old leather and wood shavings and damp where the stars gleamed through a hole in the roof.

"Over here," she said.

He went towards her, lantern raised and paused. A trick of the lamplight, he knew that, but for a moment she looked exactly as she had done down there on the road in the moonlight—as old as Eve and more beautiful than he had thought any woman could be.

She turned, leaning over the woodpile, one knee forward so that the old cotton dress tightened across her thighs like a second skin.

Five years. Five long years. Youngblood moved forward, reaching out to touch and she turned to face him. It was there in her eyes, the sudden shock, the knowing. For a moment they stayed that way and then she seemed to sway towards him.

From somewhere in the house Chavasse called, "Harry, where are you?"

Youngblood smiled, reached forward and gently stroked her face with the back of one hand. "Some other time perhaps? You take the lantern. I'll carry the wood."

She moved back clutching the lantern in both hands, the knuckles gleaming white, betraying her inner tension. Youngblood piled half a dozen logs in the crook of one arm and led the way out.

As they crossed the yard Chavasse appeared in the kitchen doorway. "So there you are? There didn't seem to be anyone around. I got worried."

"Just helping with the chores." Youngblood turned to Molly. "Where's your father got to?"

"Here I am, Mr. Youngblood." Crowther moved out of the shadows on the other side of the yard. "Just settling the animals."

"Where's Billy?"

"Never you mind about him. He sleeps in the barn. Best place for him. Are we all ready then?" He turned to the girl, rubbing his hands together and said jovially, "By gum, I don't know what you've got for us, lass, but I could eat a horse."

It was a good hour later when Billy shambled out of the darkness across the yard and approached the rear door. He opened it carefully and moved inside.

Crowther was sitting at the kitchen table smoking his pipe and reading a newspaper. He looked up and nodded calmly. "There you are then, Billy."

He went to a cupboard under the sink and came back with a ten-pound hammer. "You know what to do?"

Billy gripped the hammer tightly in his right hand and nodded eagerly, saliva glistened on his chin.

"Good lad. Best get started then."

Crowther opened the door, led the way along the passageway and mounted the stairs to the landing. He paused outside the end door, a finger on his lips and tried the knob gently. The door remained immovable and he turned calmly and pushed Billy back along the corridor.

At the bottom of the steps he paused and put a hand on the big man's shoulders. "Never mind, Billy, there's always tomorrow," he said.

In the bedroom, Chavasse and Youngblood stood in silence watching the door knob turn. When the soft footsteps had faded along the passageway, Youngblood's breath left his body in a long sigh.

"My God, I'm glad you're here," he said to Chavasse. "I feel like a ten-year-old kid that's looking for a bogie in every cupboard."

"In this house you'd probably find one. Still, there's one good thing."

"What's that?"

Chavasse grinned. "It's nice to know I'm wanted."

7

Something Nasty
in the Woodshed

Rain drifted against the window with the dismal pattering and Chavasse looked out across the farmyard morosely. In the grey light of early morning, it presented an unlovely picture. Great potholes in the cobbles filled with stagnant water, archaic, rusting machinery and a profusion of rubbish everywhere.

"Have you ever seen anything like it?" Youngblood asked in disgust. "Talk about Cannery Row."

Chavasse went to the table and poured himself another cup of tea. "What time is it?"

"Just coming up to nine forty-five."

"And Crowther said the funeral was at ten. They should be back here by half past." He nodded at the table. "Had enough to eat?"

"Yes—you fry a good egg."

Chavasse opened the kitchen door and looked up at the hill on the other side of the yard. There was a small grey stone hut on top and a scattering of grimy looking sheep.

"Think I'll take a walk—see what I can see."

Youngblood looked out over his shoulder at the rain. "Rather you than me. I'll search the house. There might be a gun around the place."

"You'll be lucky," Chavasse said. "Crowther may be primitive, but he has all the cunning of the fox."

He took an old oilskin coat down from behind the door and went outside, buttoning it up to his chin. There was a pile of rusting tin cans against the outhouse wall, the accumulation of the years, and he kicked one of them across the yard and followed it into the barn.

It was in the same state of decay as the rest of the place, planks missing from the door, rain drifting down through several holes in the roof. An old cattle truck which still seemed to be in working order was parked by the rear door and the tractor beside it, its metal parts red with rust in the damp atmosphere, looked as if it hadn't functioned for years.

Chavasse kicked the tin can carelessly out of his path. It landed in a pile of mouldy hay in one corner and a couple of brown rats shot into the open to poise in the centre of the floor watching him. *Strange how you could never get over some things.* His face wrinkled in disgust and he picked up a stone and threw it with all his force, sending them running for the shadows on the other side of the barn.

He went out through the other door, passed through a wilderness of brambles and nettles that had once been a kitchen garden and found the beginnings of a path beyond the crumbling boundary wall.

It lifted through a scattering of alder trees, following the curve of the hillside, climbing steeply to the summit. Quite suddenly he found that he was enjoying himself. There was a fine fresh smell to the rain and the hard physical exercise was something to be enjoyed for its own sake after the long weary months of prison life.

He negotiated a high drystone wall by climbing an ingenious stone stile and found himself on the final slope. Sheep wandered amongst a jumble of great boulders and outcrops of stone, carved by the winds of time into a thousand strange shapes. Above him to the rear of the hut, a clump of thorn trees stood together, their branches twisted and unnatural and pointing, like the fingers of a gnarled hand, in the same direction, forced by the prevailing wind.

The hut was larger than it had looked from the farmyard and in reasonable condition. There was fresh hay inside, dry and sweet and sacks of feedstuffs, probably for the sheep. He lit a cigarette, went back outside again, and crossed to the scattering of rocks that formed the spine of the hill.

From there he had a clear view of the main road in the valley below shrouded in mist, a gleam of water beyond. *A reservoir, perhaps a lake?* He turned away and with something of a shock, found that Molly Crowther was standing watching him.

She made a strange melancholy figure, fitting perfectly into that dead landscape in an old black coat with the padded shoulders fashionable during the war years. A scarf was bound tightly around the strong peasant face.

"Hello there," Chavasse said, walking to meet her. "Did everything go all right?"

She nodded with a curious indifference. "The

priest didn't waste much time. He was getting wet."

"Where's your father?"

"Gone into the next village with Billy. He dropped me down there on the road. It's quicker to walk over the hill and I wanted to check on the sheep."

"Do you look after them?"

"Most of the time. Billy helps me when he's in the mood. The trouble is he doesn't know his own strength. One minute he's fondling a lamb, the next its neck is broken. He isn't very reliable."

"I see your point." Chavasse hesitated and went on, "I'm sorry about your mother."

"I'm not," she said with brutal frankness. "She had cancer of the stomach during the last year of her life and refused to go to hospital. I had to look after her. It wasn't much of a time for either of us. She's well out of this place anyway."

"Don't you like it here?"

She turned on him in surprise. "Who could like a place like this?" She flung out an arm that seemed to embrace the whole wind-swept landscape. "Even the trees grow crooked here. It's a dead world. I sometimes think the only living things in it are the sheep and they're like Billy—witless."

"Why don't you leave?"

"I couldn't before—there was my mother to consider. Now it's too late. I'm squeezed dry. I wouldn't know where to go."

There was real pain in her voice and Chavasse felt genuinely sorry for her. "Perhaps your father could help. He may intend to now that your mother has gone."

"There's only one thing he wants to do for me—God knows he's tried that often enough." She laughed harshly. "My father died when I was three. He was a gypsy like my mother. She met Sam Crowther at Skipton Market ten years ago and married him within a week. The worst day's work she ever did in her life."

"You sound as if you hate him."

"And this place—all I ever wanted was to get away."

"Where would you like to go?"

"I've never really thought about it." She shrugged. "Some place where I could get a decent job, wear nice clothes, meet people—London, maybe."

From her vantage point it must have seemed as remote as the moon and just about as romantic. "Distance lends enchantment," he told her gently. "London can be the loneliest place on earth."

"I'd take my chances." They had reached one of the boundary walls and she leaned against it, arms folded under her breasts. "It must be marvelous to be able to go places—do exciting things—like Mr. Youngblood, for instance."

"Five years in gaol," Chavasse said. "Another fifteen to go if they catch him—perhaps more now. Nothing very romantic there."

"I mean before that," she said with a slight trace of impatience. "He was a smuggler, you know."

"Amongst other things."

She rushed on, looking animated for the first time since he had known her. "I read an article about him in one of the Sunday papers last year. They said he was a modern Robin Hood."

"I suppose that's one way of looking at it. Depends what the original was like."

"But it's true," she insisted. "They published an interview with an old lady who'd been treated with eviction because she couldn't pay her rent. Somebody told Mr. Youngblood. He gave her a hundred pounds and he'd never even met her before."

Chavasse could have told her that the incident had taken place just after a successful payroll snatch in Essex which was known to have netted Youngblood and his associates thirty-two thousand pounds and had put two armoured car guards in hospital, one with a fractured skull, but he knew when he was wasting his time.

He grinned crookedly. "He's certainly quite a man."

She nodded. "I hope he gets away, clear out of the country. I hope you both do."

"Do you get many people through here like us?" he said.

"About half a dozen this year."

"What about George Saxton and Ben Hoffa, Harry's friends? Did you see anything of them?"

Suddenly it was as if shutters had dropped squarely into place and when she glanced at him, the eyes were blank, the face devoid of all expression. "Yes, they were here."

"For how long?"

She hesitated and then said slowly, "I don't know. I didn't see them go."

Chavasse was aware of a sudden coldness in the pit of the stomach and his throat seemed to go dry. "Was that unusual?"

"Yes—yes, it was," she said hesitatingly. "The

others were here for two or three days. I always saw them leave. My step-father took them in the car."

"Let me get this straight," Chavasse said. "You met Saxton and Hoffa down there on the road at night just like us and you brought them up to the farm?"

"That's right."

"Did you ever see either of them again after that?"

"Never."

They stood staring at each other dumbly in the rain, the ceaseless sighing of the wind the only sound.

"What happened to them, Molly?" Chavasse said.

"I don't know. Before God, I don't know," she cried.

"You mean you don't want to know, don't you?"

She shuddered violently as if at some secret unpleasant thought and he gripped her arms above the elbows, gentling her like a fractious mare. "All right, Molly—there's nothing to worry about. I'll handle it."

He started to walk away, paused and turned towards her. "Are you coming down?"

"I've the sheep to see to." Her hands were shaking so hard that she had to clasp them together. "Later—I'll be along later."

He didn't bother to argue and went down the hill on the run, his face grim. The possibilities implicit in what she had said were monstrous and yet, if he was honest, some sort of suspicion had been there at the back of his mind from the moment he had met Sam Crowther and his sinister shadow. He remembered the knob on the bedroom door turning silently in the night and his flesh crawled.

He climbed the stone stile, vaulted the wall and found himself face to face with Youngblood.

"Find anything?" Chavasse said.

Youngblood shook his head. "Not even a shotgun. I know where we are though. Found an old envelope. This is Wykehead Farm, near Settle." He frowned suddenly. "You look excited. Anything happen?"

"I'm not really sure," Chavasse said. "But I've just had a chat with Molly and I've a hunch there could be something very nasty in the woodshed."

"What in the hell are you talking about?"

"No time to discuss it now. Ask her about Saxton and Hoffa yourself and see what you make of it. You get a clear view of the main road from the top. The moment you see Crowther's car, come down and warn me. You'll have plenty of time."

He went down the hill quickly leaving Youngblood standing there, a frown on his face. After a while he turned, climbed the stile and went up the hill.

Although he had developed, and especially in his Navy days a genuine love of the sea, Harry Youngblood was a city animal and he paused to survey the strange twisted landscape with distaste. There was nothing here that appealed to him. Nothing at all, and he climbed on until he reached the spine of rocks on the crest of the hill and looked down to the road below. A truck moved along it, match-box size, but there was no sign of Crowther's old black Ford.

He turned and started towards the hut and suddenly realised that the girl was standing there looking at him, a lamb cradled in her arms. She disappeared inside and when he reached the doorway, he found her crouched down on the floor mixing some kind of bran with milk in a feeding bowl.

"Hello there," Youngblood said. "What happened to your father?"

"He went into the next village with Billy. I came up here to check the sheep."

She had spoken without looking round and he lit a cigarette, aware of a sudden unbearable tightness in his chest that threatened to choke him. She had taken off her coat and the black woollen dress she wore was, like the cotton one of the previous night, a size too small and stretched tightly across her buttocks and thighs.

Outside, thunder echoed faintly and the rain increased with a sudden rush. She glanced briefly, almost furtively over her shoulder and again, he was conscious of that same strange trick of the light as the shadows of the hut smoothed away her plainness, softened the harshness of that strong, ugly face, making her beautiful.

She stood up, reaching to a rack on the wall and Youngblood, his throat dry, dropped his cigarette and moved close, his arms sliding around her, pulling her against him. When he turned her around, she stood there woodenly, her face expressionless, making no move to stop him as his hands crawled across her body.

Five years. Five long, hard years. Forgetting about Saxton and Hoffa and Chavasse's strange behaviour, Youngblood, hot with desire, threw every other consideration to the winds and pushed her back on to the pile of hay in the corner.

It was only when he penetrated her that she came to life, her hands tightening in his hair, her mouth fastening on his with great bruising kisses that were almost frightening in the intensity of their passion.

Below in the valley, Sam Crowther's old Ford turned off the road and started along the track to the farm.

Youngblood surfaced, his face damp with sweat and stared up at the roof. There had been no finesse about what had happened, nothing gentle and now it was over. She lay beside him, eyes closed, breasts heaving, moisture beading her upper lip and he was filled with something very close to disgust. She was ugly—God dammit, everything about her was ugly from the unkempt hair and sallow face to the dowdy black dress and darned stockings.

He eased away and she turned at once, opening her eyes. He forced a smile. "You all right, kid?"

"Oh, Harry, I love you. I love you so much." She clutched his hand and turned her face into his shoulder.

It was a cry from the heart of someone who had never known love or kindness or any kind of affection in her life before, but Youngblood had neither the perception nor the sensitivity necessary to understand, that for her he had become the only real thing in a world of illusion.

He patted her on the shoulder awkwardly and pulled away, taking out his cigarettes and lighting one. Looking for a change of subject, he remembered what Chavasse had said.

"What went on between you and Paul? When he

passed me on the way down he seemed pretty excited about something."

She got up, took a comb from the pocket of her coat and ran it through her hair. "He was asking me questions about the other people who came here, that's all."

"Like George Saxton and Ben Hoffa?"

"That's right."

"And what did he want to know?"

"If I'd seen them leave."

Youngblood frowned. "And did you?"

She shook her head. "The others who came used to stay two or three days, but I never saw either of your friends again after I brought them up here."

Youngblood stared at her in horror as the full implication sank in. "Jesus Christ!" he whispered.

In the same moment, both barrels of a shotgun were fired in rapid succession, the sound echoing flatly through the rain as it drifted up from the valley below.

He turned to the door and the girl grabbed his arm. "Don't go, Harry—don't go!" she screamed.

He struck her across the face with the flat of his hand, sending her backwards into the hay. "You bitch!" he said. "You dirty little bitch! You've sold us out!"

And then he was gone and she picked herself up and stumbled after him, crying hysterically.

When Chavasse reached the farmyard he paused, suddenly uncertain, not even sure what he was looking for. If his suspicions were correct, if Saxton and Ben Hoffa had never left this place alive, their bodies could be anywhere. Tossed into a peat bog or simply buried a foot under the surface somewhere out there on the moors, they could lie for five hundred years without being discovered.

He went inside the farmhouse and stood in the stone flagged passageway for a moment, wondering what to do next, conscious of the eerie silence. There was a door to his left and one on the right leading to the parlour and living room respectively and the kitchen was at the far end. And then he noticed another under the stairs.

When he opened it, unpleasant, dank odour drifted up to meet him from the darkness below. He fumbled for the light switch and clicked it on to disclose a flight of stone steps. He went down cautiously and found himself in a narrow white-washed passage that turned into another, various storerooms leading off on either side.

There was the usual accumulation of rubbish that was to be found in the cellars of any old house and many of the rooms had obviously been used to store provisions in other days. He was wasting his time, so much was obvious and he turned and went back along the passage.

"Doing a bit of exploring, eh?" Sam Crowther said from the top of the stairs.

He was standing in the doorway, a double-barrelled shotgun under one arm. Chavasse paused fractionally at the bottom of the steps and kept on going.

"That's right. Hope you don't mind."

"Not at all." Crowther moved back into the passageway, a jovial smile on his face. "And where's Mr. Youngblood?"

"Somewhere around."

"And Molly?" Crowther chuckled, somehow contriving to make even that sound obscene. "Happen they're together, eh?" And he dug his elbow into Chavasse's ribs.

"I wouldn't know about that."

In spite of Crowther's unctuous smile an indefinable air of menace hung around him and danger crackled in the air like electricity. Chavasse waited, tense and ready for anything that was to come, uncomfortably aware of the dull ache from his stitches, knowing that, to all intents and purposes, he might as well be one-armed.

Crowther leaned forward and winked in a conspiratorial fashion. "There's summat you might find very interesting out back, summat I wouldn't show to everybody. Seeing as how we're alone, this might just be the time."

He turned, walking ahead along the passageway and Chavasse followed him out through the kitchen. He led the way across the yard and opened a gate leading into a small courtyard. The only thing it seemed to contain was an old well surrounded by a three foot circular brick wall. Billy stood beside it, a stupid fixed grin on his ugly face, his great hands curved slightly as if he was waiting for something.

"Let's have it off then, Billy, lad." Crowther chuckled. "Nothing like a piece of female flesh for splitting the opposition. Mind you my Molly's no oil painting, I'll grant you that, but she's got the necessary and after five years inside Mr. Youngblood's not going to be too choosy now, is he?"

The barrel of the shotgun jabbed Chavasse in the back and, as the cover came off the well with a crash, he pivoted sharply, his left arm trapping the barrel against his side, the edge of his right hand slashing Crowther across the side of the neck so that he cried out in pain and staggered back.

Chavasse pulled the shotgun from under his armpit with his right hand, thumbing back the hammers awkwardly as he ran for the gate. As he started to turn, Billy gave a cry of rage and lurched forward.

He was like some primeval beast lumbering in for the kill, the nightmare face contorted with rage, great hands outstretched to rend and tear. Chavasse didn't even let him get close. He swung up the shotgun one-handed, resting the barrels across his left arm and fired. The first shot caught Billy in the chest, stopping him dead in his tracks, the second blew away half his face, scattering blood and brain across the cobblestones, driving him back against the well. He hit the wall, jack-knifed and disappeared without a cry. There was a single splash and then silence.

Crowther lay on his face moaning softly and Chavasse dropped to one knee beside him and searched his pockets. He found a handful of cartridges and reloaded the shotgun, then he gave Crowther a kick in the ribs and stood back.

"On your feet."

Crowther scrambled up, backing against the wall of the courtyard. Chavasse moved in and rammed the muzzle of the shotgun under the man's chin.

"Saxton and Hoffa, they're down there, aren't they?" Crowther hesitated and the muzzle dug painfully into his flesh. "Aren't they?"

Crowther nodded fearfully. "That's right."

"How many more?" Again he hesitated and Chavasse thumbed back the hammers of the shotgun.

"For God's sake, don't shoot!" Crowther cried. "Four—that's all."

"That's all," Chavasse said in disgust, fighting back the inclination to pull the trigger. "Then other people were passed through safely?"

"That's right. I was only obeying orders."

"I bet you were. The people you passed on? Where did they go to next?"

"I wouldn't know." The barrel of the shotgun was raised menacingly and he cried out in alarm. "It's the truth, I tell you. I used to drop them ten miles from here at a crossroads to be picked up by someone else."

There was the sound of running feet and Youngblood called through the rain from the house. "Drum—where are you?"

"Out here!" Chavasse replied.

Youngblood arrived a moment later and paused in the gateway. "What happened here?"

"They thought I might be more comfortable down the well, but Billy decided to try it instead. You'll be interested to know that's where Saxton and Ben Hoffa are."

Youngblood crossed to Crowther. "You dirty bastard."

Very slowly, but with infinite menace, he searched the older man, tossing the contents of his pockets carelessly onto the cobbles. He found a wallet which appeared to contain fifty or sixty pounds and nodded to Chavasse.

"This should be useful. What's he told you?"

"Everybody didn't end up down the well. Most of the clients were passed on."

"Where to?"

"He doesn't know. Says he drops them at a cross-roads about ten miles from here to be picked up."

Youngblood turned on Crowther and laughed harshly. "Are you trying to tell me you never hung around to see what happened, never followed any-body? In a pig's ear, you didn't."

He sank his fist into the pit of Crowther's stom-ach so that he screamed and doubled over, falling to his knees. A foot caught him a glancing blow on the shin and he fell over backwards.

"Now try him," Youngblood said.

Chavasse dropped on one knee beside Crowther and raised his head. "He means business—I'd talk if I were you."

Crowther nodded, a dazed expression in his eyes and wiped blood from his cheek. "All right, I'll tell you. I did follow clients twice."

"What happened?"

"They were picked up by a furniture van and dropped off on the outskirts of Shrewsbury."

"Then what?"

"They waited on a certain bench and were picked up by the same person each time—a blind woman with a guide dog. Her name's Hartman—Rosa Hartman and she lives at Alma Cottage, Bampton. She's some sort of a clairvoyante."

At that moment, the girl arrived, panting and out of breath, her face flushed. She poised in the gate-way and looked around her wildly.

"Are you all right, Harry?"

Youngblood turned and went towards her. "If I

am, it's no thanks to you, you rotten little bitch. I could have been at the bottom of that well by tonight and no questions asked."

She was crying, her face looking uglier than ever and pawed at his chest. "I didn't know, Harry. I didn't know."

"Do you think I came over on a banana boat or something?" Youngblood said and he grabbed her hair viciously, wrenching back her head.

Chavasse moved across the courtyard in three quick strides and pulled him away. "Leave her alone, Harry. She'd nothing to do with it. All she ever had were suspicions and if she hadn't mentioned those, I probably wouldn't be here now."

Behind them, Crowther saw his chance and ran for a gap in the wall where the brickwork had crumbled. Youngblood turned with a cry of alarm, but he was too late and Chavasse grabbed his arm to hold him back as Crowther ran for his life through the undergrowth on the other side of the wall.

"Never mind him—we've got to get out of here."

They went out into the main courtyard and the girl plucked at Youngblood's sleeve. "You'll take me with you, Harry?"

"Do me a favour," Youngblood said and pushed her away violently.

"But you can't leave me," she pleaded. "Not now."

"What's she talking about?" Chavasse demanded.

"How the hell should I know?" Youngblood said impatiently. "I'll get some food from the house and we'll get moving. I suppose we'd better take the Ford."

"Please Harry!"

The girl was crying bitterly and Chavasse looked at her, a frown on his face. He didn't like leaving her, if only because Crowther might return. On the other hand she would be nothing but a hindrance. *Or would she?*

He put a hand on her shoulder. "Molly, can you drive?"

She looked up eagerly. "Of course I can."

"What are you up to?" Youngblood demanded

"I was just thinking," Chavasse said. "What if we run into a road block somewhere. It's always possible. If the girl drove a mile in front in the Ford and we followed in the cattle truck, there'd be time for her to turn back and warn us."

Youngblood nodded slowly. "You know, I think you've got something there." He turned to Molly and put a hand on her shoulder. "Think you can do it, kid?"

She gazed up at him, an expression of pure joy in her eyes. "Just try me, Harry. Just try me."

Five minutes after the truck had rolled away down the track, Sam Crowther emerged from the trees at the back of the farm and limped across the yard. His mouth was badly swollen and his chest hurt so that he could hardly breathe.

He leaned over the sink, holding his head under the cold tap and when he straightened, reaching for a towel, he found Simon Vaughan standing in the open doorway.

"Hello, Mr. Smith," Crowther said uncertainly. "I didn't expect to see you."

"Just thought I'd look in to see if everything had

gone off smoothly," Vaughan said. "You look as if you've been in the wars, old man."

"Nothing I couldn't handle." Crowther's brain worked overtime. "You've brought the money with you, I hope."

"You've disposed of them already?" Vaughan said. "I must say that's very efficient of you. Where are they?"

"In the well at the rear."

"Mind if we take a look?"

Crowther hesitated. "You won't see much. Still— suit yourself."

It was still raining when they went into the court-yard and approached the well. The stench was appalling, but such was the depth of the shaft that it was impossible to see what lay at the bottom.

"So you put them down there, did you?" Vaughan said.

"That's right."

Vaughan sighed. "You know you really are the most awful liar. I've just walked over the hill, old man. I saw Youngblood and Drummond drive away in that cattle truck of yours."

Which was true, although he had missed Molly's departure in the Ford by five minutes.

"You have a daughter, don't you? Where is she?"

"I reckon she's cleared off," Crowther whispered.

"I see. Did you tell our friends about Alma Cottage at Bampton and Rosa Hartman?" Crowther's face was his answer and he shook his head gently. "You shouldn't have done that, old man. You really shouldn't."

His right hand came out of his pocket and swung up, the blade of a flicked knife springing into view, the point catching Crowther under the chin and shearing through the roof of his mouth into his brain.

He died instantly and Vaughan pulled out the knife, holding him upright, cleaned the blade carefully on Crowther's jacket, then pushed him over the wall into the well. He turned and walked away through the rain whistling tunelessly.

8

Distant Thunder

Vaughan passed the cattle truck within fifteen
miles, travelling fast in a green Triumph Spitfire. A
mile further on he overtook the old black Ford with
Molly at the wheel, but it meant nothing to him. He
had never met Crowther's stepdaughter and had
certainly no reason to think she was in any way
linked with the fugitives.

On the other side of Blackburn, he pulled in at a
roadside cafe, found a telephone box and called
World Wide Exports in London.

"Hello, sweetie, just thought I'd let you know I
checked on our friend and he hadn't managed to
come up to scratch. I'm afraid the two packages are
on their way to Bampton."

"That's a great pity. What are you doing about
it?"

"I closed our account with this branch—seemed
no point in carrying on and I can be in Bampton
before the merchandise. Thought I'd ensure it gets
a suitable reception."

"I'm not certain that's such a good idea. I'd bet

er check. Give me your number and I'll ring back
n fifteen minutes."

Vaughan left the phone box, sat on the high stool
t the counter and ordered coffee. The young wait-
ess smiled when she gave it to him, impressed by
he handsome stranger in the expensive clothes, but
Vaughan seemed to look right through her and she
moved away feeling rather disappointed.

He lit a cigarette and frowned at himself in the
mirror at the back of the counter. It was not that he
was remembering what had happened at the
arm—he had already dismissed it from his mind as
unimportant. He was only interested in what lay
ahead, in whether the Baron would decide that he
wanted him to dispose of Youngblood and Drummond personally.

Simon Vaughan was thirty-three years of age,
he son of a regular army colonel whose wife had
deserted him when the boy was eight months old.
From then on life had been a long round of other
people's houses, boarding schools and army sta-
ions abroad for short periods. He had developed
into a handsome, smiling boy, strangely lacking in
any kind of emotional response to life, but pleasant
nd popular with everyone.

After Sandhurst he was commissioned into the
Parachute Regiment and the first rather unpleasant
incident had occurred. Lieutenant Vaughan's
fanatical insistence on discipline and hard training
ad included the use of pack drill to punish those
who failed to meet his standards. In spite of the
physical collapse of four men and a slashing report
rom the battalion medical officer, he had escaped
with only a reprimand.

In Cyprus he had been awarded the Military
Cross for personally killing two EOKA members
who had holed up in a farmhouse in a village in the
Troodos and had defied all attempts to get them
out. He had gone in through the roof and had shot it
out at close quarters in a manner which had certainly left no doubts about his personal courage
although the discovery that the two insurgents had
only one gun between them had left uneasy doubts
in some quarters.

These were finally confirmed when Vaughan, by
then a captain, was once again in action, this time
in the Radfan Mountains of Southern Arabia
playing a savage game of hide-and-seek with dissi-
dent Yemeni tribesmen. In an effort to extrac
information from a Bedouin, Vaughan had pegged
him out in the sun and employed methods more
popular amongst the tribesmen themselves than
the British. The man had died, Vaughan had been
relieved of his command and quietly retired to
avoid any scandal.

His father, acting on the advice of the army med
ical authorities, had persuaded him to enter a pri
vate institution for rest and treatment, but afte
two weeks Vaughan walked out, disappearing of
the face of the earth as far as his family was con
cerned.

The psychiatrists had experienced little difficulty
in making their diagnosis. Simon Vaughan was a
psychopath—a mental cripple, a man who wa
incapable of any ordinary emotion, who lived out
side any moral frame of reference whatsoever. The
taking of human life affected him no more than
would the crushing of an ant underfoot by any aver

age human being. He was the perfect weapon—a blunt instrument with a brilliant and incisive mind and the work he engaged in for his present employer suited his talents admirably.

A middle-aged woman came into the cafe, ordered a coffee and made for the phone box. Vaughan beat her to it, removing his hat and giving her his most charming smile.

"Would you mind awfully if I asked you to hang on for a minute or two? I'm expecting a call."

The woman smiled, her heart fluttering unaccountably, and put a hand to her hair. "Not at all."

"So kind."

Vaughan was still smiling at her through the glass when the phone rang and he picked it up instantly. "Hello, sweetie, what's the good word?"

"Carry on to Bampton and ensure that the merchandise is forwarded to our contact in Gloucester. Give him a ring and tell him what to expect."

"The full treatment?"

"Absolutely. And Simon, he doesn't want you to get involved personally unless it becomes absolutely necessary. If the occasion calls for it, then you have a free hand, but for the moment, simply keep an eye on things and report progress."

"Will do, sweetie."

He came out of the phone box and smiled cheerfully at the middle-aged woman. "Terribly sorry if I've held you up. You must allow me to put your coffee on my check."

She blushed like a young girl. "That isn't necessary—really it isn't."

"Oh, but I insist."

He left a generous tip and went out, whistling

softly and the woman sighed and said to the girl behind the counter, "It isn't often you meet young men with manners like that these days."

The girl nodded. "Still, he's a real gentleman, isn't he? Anyone can see that."

Outside, Vaughan gunned the motor of the Spitfire and drove rapidly away.

The needle on the speedometer of the old cattle truck obstinately refused to move past thirty-five and it was coming up half past three when they approached Bampton.

Chavasse tapped Youngblood on the shoulder and pointed to where Molly stood beside the old Ford in a lay-by and Youngblood drew in beside her. It was raining hard, but there was colour in her cheeks and she seemed cheerful and excited when he dropped down to join her.

"How did it go, kid?"

"Fine," she said. "No trouble at all."

He turned to Chavasse who came round the front of the truck. "What was that address again?"

"Alma Cottage."

"Could be anywhere."

"True—Molly had better go in on her own. We don't want to make ourselves too conspicuous."

Youngblood nodded, took out Crowther's wallet and extracted five pounds. "You must be running low on petrol. Fill her right up while you're at it and get me some cigarettes and a newspaper if you can."

She drove away quickly into the heavy rain and the two men climbed back into the cab of the cattle truck.

"No road blocks so far, that's one good thing," Youngblood said.

Chavasse shrugged. "We're more than two hundred miles away from Fridaythorpe now. They aren't looking for us here—not yet anyway."

"Then there was no need to trail along in this old crate," Youngblood said. "We could have ditched the girl and used the Ford."

Chavasse managed to restrain his anger with difficulty. "Maybe you'd prefer to wander round Bampton showing your face all over the place while you try to find Alma Cottage?" he said. "Not me. If we aren't spread across page one by now then we ought to be." He shook his head. "She's earning her keep as far as I'm concerned."

"Maybe you're right at that," Youngblood said grudgingly.

"You can put money on it."

Chavasse sprawled back in the passenger seat, smoked one of his last cigarettes and went over things in his mind. So far, so good. Crowther's treachery to his employers—the fact that he had followed clients through to the Bampton address—had been a major stroke of luck. Without it, they wouldn't have stood a chance and the whole business, the long weary months in prison, would have been all for nothing.

But what happened now was even more important. He wondered just how much Rosa Hartman, the blind woman Crowther had mentioned, had to tell them. Possibly very little.

The Ford appeared round a bend in the road and drew in beside them. When Molly got out, she was carrying a carton of cigarettes and a newspaper.

"Alma Cottage is on this side of the village," she said. "I've just driven past it. There's a narrow lane on the right hand side of the road. It's about two hundred yards beyond the bend. The cottage is almost half-way along. It's very pretty."

Youngblood opened the newspaper and his face seemed to jump out to meet him. It wasn't a prison photo, but one taken at the time of his trial on the steps of the courthouse and he smiled out at the crowd, one hand raised in a careless wave.

On the evidence of that photo alone, thousands of ordinary people throughout the country had thought him hard done by, just as today they must be hoping in their hearts that he would escape.

"Not bad, eh?" Youngblood said, unable to keep an edge of pride out of his voice. "We're making the bastards sit up and take notice."

It was still there. The old need for notoriety at any price, the same subconscious urge towards self destruction, but Chavasse said nothing. Beneath Youngblood's picture there was one of himself, but much smaller.

Youngblood chuckled. "They've almost missed you out, Drum. It doesn't even look like you."

Chavasse shook his head. "You can have all the publicity you want, Harry. As far as I'm concerned, I won't be happy till we're both a three-line story at the end of column eight on page twelve."

"And that won't be for a week at least. These newspaper boys know a good story when they see one." Youngblood folded the paper and tossed it into the cab of the cattle truck. "Anyway, let's get moving."

"I've been thinking about that," Chavasse said.

"We could run into trouble—no way of telling. Silly for both of us to go."

"Fair enough." Youngblood grinned and put an arm around the girl. "I'll stay here and look after Molly."

"Suits me," Chavasse said calmly. "If I'm not back in an hour you'd better come looking."

"If I'm still here," Youngblood said sardonically.

Chavasse nodded. "Come to think of it, that does seem to be a distinct possibility. Under the circumstances I'll have half the bank roll—just in case I have to fend for myself."

Youngblood hesitated perceptibly and then produced Crowther's wallet. "Why not?" He counted out twenty-five pounds and gave it to Chavasse together with a handful of loose change. "And how do I know you won't decide to take off on your own?"

"You don't," Chavasse said and he turned and walked away quickly through the heavy rain.

Youngblood looked down at the girl who gazed up at him shyly. Her face was wet with the rain, the eyes shining. Strangely enough, she didn't look half bad and he slipped his arm around her waist and squeezed gently.

"Come on, kid, we could have a long wait. Might as well get into the back of the truck and make ourselves comfortable."

"All right, Harry."

She moved ahead of him and when he helped her up over the tailboard, his hands were shaking with excitement.

The cottage stood well back from the lane, an old

grey-stone building half-covered by ivy. The long narrow garden was wet with rain, the only flowers a few early daffodils and he went along the flagged path to the porch. A brass plate at one side of the door said *Madame Rosa Hartman—consultations by appointment only.*

Chavasse knocked. There was a sudden patter of feet inside like wind through dry leaves, a low growl and then silence. After a while he heard the tapping of a stick, the door swung open and a woman looked out at him.

She was at least seventy, her hair drawn back from a yellowing parchment face in an old-fashioned bun. She wore a tweed suit with a skirt which almost reached her ankles and carried an ebony cane in her left hand. Her right hand had a secure grip on the collar of one of the most superb dogs Chavasse had ever seen in his life—a black and tan Dobermann.

A growl started deep down in its throat like distant thunder and she jerked hard on the collar. "Be quiet, Karl. Yes, who is it?"

She had spoken with a slight Austrian accent and as she leaned forward, he got a clear look at the cloudy opalescent eyes.

"I was wondering if you could spare me a few moments of your time."

"You wish to consult me professionally?"

"That's right."

"I only take clients by appointment. I have to be very careful. The law is most strict in these matters."

"I'm only passing through," he said. "I'd really

be most obliged. You were very highly recommended."

"I see." She appeared to hesitate. "Your name?"

"Is of no importance," he said. "Only my destination."

"And what would that be?"

"Babylon!"

There was a moment of stillness and then she moved back slightly. "I think you'd better come in, young man."

The hall was oak panelled and very pleasant with hyacinths growing in a bowl on a polished table that stood before a long gilt mirror. She closed the door, releasing her hold on the Dobermann and the dog moved to Chavasse's side.

"This way," she said and walked to a door at the other end of the hall.

The room was obviously a study with books lining the walls, but a cheerful fire burned in an Adam grate and through the diamond paned window, he glimpsed trees through the rain and a river beyond.

The woman sat on the other side of a small round table and indicated the vacant chair opposite. Chavasse took it and the Dobermann subsided on the floor, its eyes fixed on his unwinkingly.

"Who are you, young man?" Rosa Hartman said.

"Does that matter?"

She shrugged. "Perhaps not. Give me your hand."

Chavasse was momentarily bewildered. "Might I ask why?"

"For me, it is always necessary. I am clairvoyante, surely you were aware of that?"

He took her hand, holding it lightly. It was cool

and flaccid, making him remember for no accountable reason, his Breton grandmother, clean linen sheets, rosemary and lavender and then she tightened her grip and he was aware of a sudden tingle as from a minor electric shock. The strange thing was that suddenly, her eyes widened and she reached out and ran the fingers of her free hand lightly over his face.

"Is anything wrong?" he asked.

She shook her head, still frowning. "I expected something a little different, that's all." She held his hand a moment longer and then released it. "Who sent you here?"

"Does that matter?"

"No, you have the password, but I was not expecting you."

"Then you can't help?"

She spread her hands in a vaguely continental gesture. "No arrangements have been made to take you to the next stage. There is no transport ready."

"I have transport."

"I see—you are alone?"

He hesitated. "Yes."

The strange creamy eyes seemed to gaze through him and beyond so that he knew instantly that she was aware that he had lied.

"You can help me then?"

"Yes—yes, I think so. At least I can show you where to go. Whether that will give you what you are looking for is something else again."

It was as if in some strange way she was trying to warn him and he smiled. "I'll take my chances."

"Then go to the desk behind you and open the top right hand drawer beneath the pigeon holes. You will find several copies of the same visiting card. Take one. I should add that I do not know what is on the card nor do I wish to know."

Chavasse got up and the dog stirred uneasily. He ignored it, walked to the desk and opened the drawer she had indicated. The visiting card was edged in black and carried the legend:

Long Barrow Crematorium and House of Rest— Hugo Pentecost—Director, in neat Gothic script. The phone number was Phenge 239.

"Now please go, young man," Rosa Hartman said.

Chavasse paused, frowning, the card between his fingers. There was something wrong here— something very wrong and then the dog stood up and growled softly. Chavasse took a cautious step backwards. If there was one dog on earth capable of killing a man, it was a Dobermann Pincher. Once launched on target, only a machine gun would stop it.

"You can let yourself out," she said. "Karl will see you to the door."

The Dobermann moved forward at once as if it understood every word she said and Chavasse took the hint. "I'd like to thank you, Madam Hartman. You've been of very real assistance to me."

"That remains to be seen, young man," she said calmly. "Now go."

There was a public telephone box at the end of the lane and he went inside and dialled Bureau headquarters in London quickly. He was through within a matter of seconds and asked for Mallory. A moment later, Janet Frazer's voice sounded on the line.

"I'm afraid Mr. Mallory isn't available. This is his secretary speaking. Can I help?"

"Janet—Paul here." There was a sudden sharp intake of breath at the other end. "Where is he?"

"Foreign Office—a NATO intelligence conference. Where are you?"

"Shrewsbury and hot on the trail. Ever heard of a place called Phenge?"

"No, but I can soon look it up for you." She was back within a couple of minutes. "Just outside Gloucester."

"That's where we're making for now. The whole thing's going perfectly so far. From now on I must have Mallory standing by. Next time I ring, it could be to give him the news he's been waiting for and I'll probably only have seconds."

"I'll tell him."

"Good girl. I'll have to be off."

"Look after yourself."

"Don't worry about me. I'll challenge the gods and make a date with you for next Wednesday. We'll do a show and go on to the Saddle Room afterwards."

"I'll look forward to that."

He dropped the receiver and hurried along the road through the heavy rain. When he reached the lay-by, the girl was sitting in the van and Youngblood was standing by the truck smoking. He moved to meet Chavasse quickly.

"What happened?"

"Nothing much. She gave me this card."

Youngblood read it and looked up quickly. "Was she on the level?"

"How in the hell would I know?"

"Then we could be walking into trouble."

"Naturally."

Youngblood nodded thoughtfully. "On the other hand they're not going to scream for a copper, are they? That's the last thing they'll want to do."

"Exactly," Chavasse said. "Which makes it a nice private fight."

There was an old A.A. book in the Ford and Youngblood leafed through it quickly. "Phenge is just outside Gloucester," he announced. "That's about seventy-five miles. We could be there in a couple of hours if we used the Ford."

"Just what I was thinking," Chavasse said. "I noticed a gate barring a cart track into a wood a little way back. If we ran the truck in there, it could stand for a day or two before anyone discovered it, especially in this weather."

"Fine," Youngblood said. "I'll handle this. You follow on in the Ford."

He was suddenly like a kid on an outing, cheerful and smiling as he clambered up into the truck and drove away.

"He's certainly pleased with life, isn't he?" Chavasse said as he slid behind the wheel of the Ford.

The girl blushed, looking for a moment almost pretty and he was suddenly reminded of an old Breton saying. *Love makes even an ugly woman beautiful*. . . .

My God, as if this business wasn't complicated

enough. He sighed heavily as he released the
handbrake and drove away.

As the front door closed behind Chavasse, Simon
Vaughan stepped from behind the floor length velvet curtain at the window and came towards the
table.

"Glad you were sensible, old girl. I think the
whole thing went off very well, don't you?"

"That depends entirely on your point of view."

"He was lying of course—about being on his own
I mean. That was quite obvious. I suppose Youngblood was waiting at the end of the lane to see what
happened. Do you mind if I use the phone?"

"You used me. How can I stop you using my
phone?"

"Now don't be like that." He dialled a number
long distance on STD and cut in the moment he
heard a voice at the other end. "Hugo? Just to con-
firm your two packages are on the way. Yes, the full
treatment. I'll see you later."

He put down the telephone, took out his gloves
and pulled them on. "I must be off. I'll be seeing
you, Rosa."

The Dobermann brushed past him like a dark
shadow and nuzzled her hand. She shook her head.
"I don't think so."

"Now don't be silly," he said. "You've been living here on a false passport since 1946—on a false
identity, which is even worse. A word in the right
quarter . . ."

"You mistake me," she said. "It isn't that I've
grown brave all of a sudden. I'm too old for the kind

of courage that would take. I simply meant that *you* wouldn't be seeing me again."

He was obviously curious. "May I ask why?"

"Because you are going to die," she said simply.

He stared at her, that slight fixed smile firmly in place. "You really mean that, don't you?"

"I have another kind of sight, Mr. Smith or whatever your name is. Death has already marked you out. I can feel it."

And he believed her, that was the strange thing. She knew quite suddenly that he believed her completely and a shiver ran down her spine as he started to laugh.

"You're bad luck, old woman. Why shouldn't I send you on before me?"

He produced the spring blade knife with which he had murdered Crowther and the blade jumped out of his fist with an audible click.

The Dobermann growled, the hair lifting on its neck and she patted it soothingly. "Because Karl would kill you first."

"Proving your prediction in the process? What an admirable pet." Vaughan chuckled as he folded the knife and slipped it back into his pocket. "No, Rosa, we mustn't make it too easy for you. Death must find me—I'll not go looking for him. We've met before. He knows my face."

She heard him go along the corridor outside, whistling tunelessly to himself and the door banged. Somewhere, a small trapped wind circled the room looking for a way out, then died in a corner.

9

Ashes to Ashes

It was very quiet in the embalming room and Hugo Pentecost worked alone, his rubber apron smeared with blood. There was no need for him to engage in the more practical work of the establishment, but he liked to keep his hand in and in any case, there was always a certain pleasure to be derived from a job well done.

The cadaver on which he was engaged was that of a young woman and he was in the process of withdrawing her viscera. It was usual to wear rubber gloves, but Pentecost never could, preferring the additional sensitivity to be found in bare hands.

He had successfully removed the contents of the abdomen and was now on the throat, whistling softly, his arms dappled with blood up to the elbows.

The door opened behind him and a tall gaunt man with sunken cheeks and dull eyes came in. Like Pentecost he wore a heavy rubber apron.

"Anything I can do, Mr. Pentecost?"

"I'm all through here for tonight, George," Pentecost said. "Her cranium will have to wait till tomorrow. I've got rather a lot of paperwork to get through. Help me put her in the tank, will you?"

He hosed the body down quickly, flushing away the blood and they lifted her between them into a large glass tank of formaldehyde. The body slid under the surface with a soft splash and turned over several times before settling a foot or so from the bottom, the long hair fanning out in a most lifelike manner.

"A shame, isn't it, Mr. Pentecost?" George said. "She was really beautiful."

"Beautiful or ugly, young or old, this is what they all come down to in the end, George," Pentecost said cheerfully. "Has everyone else gone?"

"Yes, sir."

"No need for you to hang around. As I said, I'll be here for quite some time."

"I'll go then, if that's all right with you, Mr. Pentecost. I did promise to take my wife out for a meal."

"Try the Golden Dragon on Michener Street," Pentecost advised. "They do a really excellent Chow Mein."

"Well, thank you, sir. I think we will."

George withdrew and Pentecost went to the sink and washed the blood from his arms. He removed his rubber apron, went into the private bathroom at the other end of the embalming room, stripped and showered. The warm water made him feel pleasantly relaxed and afterwards, he stood in front of the mirror, humming softly as he changed into a soft white shirt, black tie and a beautifully tailored suit in dark worsted.

With his snow white hair and gold rimmed spectacles, he looked remarkably as one might have expected the director of Long Barrow Crematorium and House of Rest to look. Certainly there was no resemblance to Harry Marks, the second rate confidence man who had served three terms of imprisonment as a young man before learning the facts of life.

Things were very different now and he went through the embalming room and moved along the corridor, his feet silent on the thick carpets. An indefinable aura of dignity pervaded the whole establishment, there was no question of that. There was polished wood and brass everywhere and flowers and cut glass winking in the soft light from the shaded lamps.

Which was as it should be. This was, after all, the last earthly resting place for so many people. Strange that its fortunes should have been founded on murder, morally at least, although a court of law would probably have found that there was no case to answer.

Poor Alice Tisdale, on the other hand, might have thought otherwise. A lonely old widow of seventy with a pension and £13,000 in the bank, she had been captivated by the considerate stranger who had offered her his umbrella one rainy morning on the front at Brighton.

Once installed as chauffeur and general handyman at the house in Forest Hill, Harry Marks had put into operation a programme scientifically designed to break first the old woman's spirit and then her health. She had died of the combined effects of malnutrition and senile decay leaving faithful Harry all she possessed and the two cousins and a nephew who had attempted to contest the will got nowhere.

But Harry Marks belonged to another world. Now there was only Hugo Pentecost and Long Barrow, had been at least until the arrival of Smith the previous year with his quiet, cultured voice and distressingly accurate knowledge of Harry Marks and his past activities. So, when the whip cracked, he had to jump. Still, one could only be philosophical about these things and life had an interesting habit of turning full circle. His chance would come and when it did. . . .

As he went down the beautiful marble staircase he was thinking of the new incinerator, installed only the previous week, which could consume a human body in fifteen minutes. Not like the older ones which took up to an hour and a half and were so inefficient that it was usually necessary to pound up the skull and pelvis afterwards. Come to think of it, Smith wasn't particularly big. It would probably take no longer than ten minutes in his case.

As he crossed the foyer at the bottom of the stairs and walked towards his office, he became aware of a young woman standing at the reception desk.

She turned awkwardly. "I'm looking for Mr. Pentecost."

"I am he. What can I do for you?"

Pentecost's habitually soft tones carried a sharper edge than usual. The young woman was plain—in fact, rather ugly. He could have forgiven her for that, but the shabby coat and poor quality shoes, the scarf bound round the head peasant-fashion, reminded him too much for his peace of mind, of a childhood spent amidst the poverty of Whitechapel. And then there was her voice with its broad northern vowels—an accent which had always offended him.

"It was a relative I really wanted to see you about. My great aunt."

"She has just passed on?"

"This morning. I'd like to arrange for her to be taken care of. You are Mr. Hugo Pentecost?"

"Yes, I am he." Mr. Pentecost sighed. "My dear child, you have my deepest condolences, but I must point out that we offer a very specialised service here and one that is rather expensive."

Searching desperately for an answer to keep the conversation going, Molly remembered her own mother's recent death and something Crowther had mentioned.

"There was an insurance."

"May I ask how much?"

"Two hundred pounds. Would that be enough?"

Pentecost warmed to her, his voice deepening appreciably and he placed an arm around her shoulders. "I'm sure we can manage something. Perhaps you could return in the morning."

"I'd hoped to settle things tonight. Is it too late?"

"My staff have all gone home. I'm completely alone here." He hesitated and greed won. "But why not? It won't take long to settle the essential details. Come into my office."

He opened the door and showed her inside. It was furnished in excellent if rather sombre taste and he motioned her to a chair and sat down behind his desk.

He opened a large desk diary, produced a black

and gold fountain pen. "Just a few details—your name?"

"Crowther—Molly Crowther."

"Address?"

"I'm not sure." He looked up with a frown and Molly said hesitatingly, "It's on the road that leads to Babylon."

In the silence which followed, he sat staring at her, his slight polite smile wiped away. "I see."

He closed the desk diary, opened a drawer and put it away, at the same time taking out a .38 revolver with his other hand and slipping it into his pocket, an act which completely escaped the girl's notice.

He stood up. "Would you kindly come this way?"

Molly got to her feet, panic moving inside her. She hadn't the slightest idea what to do next and reached out to touch his arm timidly as he brushed past her.

"There's nothing to worry about," Pentecost said reassuringly. "We'll talk upstairs."

She followed him up the stairway and along the quiet corridor at the top. He paused outside a leather covered door, opened it and stood back for her.

The room was a place of shadows and she moved inside uncertainly. The first thing she noticed was the heavy smell of formaldehyde and then she saw the body floating in the tank tinged with green in the subdued light, hair trailing like seaweed. Her throat went dry and she turned with a gasp as the door clicked shut.

Pentecost paused beside a bench to open a large mahogany case of surgical instruments. He selected a razor sharp scalpel and held it up to the light, examining the edge of the blade with a slight frown. Quite suddenly he reached out, grabbing her by the coat, pulling her so close that their faces were only an inch or two apart. The smoothness, the suavity had disappeared—even the voice had changed as he touched the edge of the blade to her skin.

"I don't know what in the hell you're playing at, but there should be two of you, that I do know. Where's your friend? Quick now or I'll slice your throat."

And Molly, pushed beyond endurance, shoved him away wildly and screamed.

The Ford was parked in the shadows beneath a clump of beech trees a hundred yards up the road from the main gate of the Long Barrow estate.

Through the trees, Youngblood could see the dim bulk of the house, a light shining in the porch. It was the sort of Gothic pile built on the high tide of Victorian prosperity by some self-made pillar of Empire. In the darkness and rain, it was impossible to see much of the grounds, but from the size of the house, they were obviously extensive.

Footsteps approached through the darkness and Chavasse joined him. "According to the notice on the gate the place closes at six. What time is it now?"

Youngblood checked the luminous dial of his watch. "Six-fifteen."

"Someone drove out while I was down there, but there's still a car parked in front of the house. I could see it from the gate. A Mercedes from the look of it."

"Only the boss man could run a car like that," Youngblood said.

"That sounds logical." Chavasse frowned. "I still feel something stinks about this whole thing."

"Maybe you're right," Youngblood said impatiently, "but where does that get us? We've got to take a chance. We don't have any choice."

"Perhaps you're right, but I always like to hedge my bets." Chavasse leaned in at the window of the Ford and said to the girl, "You could help a lot here, Molly. Like to try?"

"Anything," she said, getting out into the rain. "Just tell me what you want me to do."

"Walk right up to the front door and ask for Hugo Pentecost. Once you're alone with him, spin him some yarn. Tell him your great aunt's died and you want to arrange cremation. At some point in the conversation introduce the word Babylon. I don't care how you do it so long as you say the word. His reaction should be very interesting."

"What about us?" Youngblood demanded.

"We'll take a look from a different direction. I'll try the back of the house, you the front or one of the sides." Chavasse turned to Molly. "We'll be right behind you, Molly. Think you can handle it?"

She nodded and Youngblood moved close to her. "Don't worry, kid. If he lays a finger on you I'll break his back."

They were empty words, brash and arrogant and yet she reached out to clutch his arm at once. "I know I can rely on you, Harry."

Even Youngblood could not avoid what was implicit in that remark and there was a kind of uncertainty in his voice as he patted her on the

shoulder awkwardly and replied, "Just yell if yo
need me and I'll come running."

Chavasse could have laughed out loud if th
whole thing hadn't been so damned tragic. In an
case, there was no time for tears and he took com
mand with an assumed briskness.

"Let's get moving. You go straight up the drive t
the front door, Molly and remember what I said–
we'll be right behind you."

The rain passed through the trees with a grea
rushing sound and Chavasse and Youngblood stoo
in the shadows by the gate and watched her moun
the steps into the porch. Beyond, through a wall c
glass, lay the deserted foyer and she pushed ope
the door and moved towards the reception desk.

Chavasse turned to Youngblood quickly. "That
it. I'll go round to the rear. You look after thing
from this end."

He disappeared into the trees and Youngbloo
walked toward the house, keeping to the shelter c
rhododendron bushes that grew in such profusio
on one side of the drive.

He could still see right into the glass-fronte
entrance hall and suddenly, a man came down th
stairs, dark-suited and with striking white hair. H
stood talking to Molly for a moment or two an
Youngblood crouched in the shadows and waited
After a while, they moved through a door to the le
and he got to his feet and went closer.

He stood in the shadows at the bottom of th
steps and waited behind one of the pillars. Within
few minutes, the door opened and Molly and th
white haired man came out and went upstairs.

Youngblood stood there, a frown on his face, wondering what to do next, realising for the first time, and with a kind of wonder, that up until now, Drummond seemed to have been making all the decisions. It was something as prosaic as a sudden increase in the force of the rain that decided him. He ran up the steps quickly, pushed open the heavy glass door and went inside.

It was as quiet as the grave and he hesitated for a moment and then crossed the foyer and went up the marble stairs. He reached the landing above and had only taken a couple of steps along it when Molly screamed.

Youngblood turned instinctively to run and then she screamed again and this time called his name. Perhaps what happened next was a reflex action—perhaps it was a product of pride or even shame or of the colossal vanity that knowing her good opinion, refused to let her find him wanting.

He flung open the leather-covered door and went in crouching, aware only fleetingly of the macabre backdrop to what was taking place. Pentecost had Molly back across the bench, a hand at her throat, the scalpel raised threateningly.

As she screamed again, Youngblood grabbed Pentecost by the shoulder, swung him round and knocked him backwards across the bench. The girl flung herself into his arms, her face twisted and ugly with fear and as he patted her reassuringly, Pentecost scrambled to his feet and pulled the revolver from his pocket.

The first clear emotion that exploded in Youngblood's brain was one of anger at his own stupidity in getting involved, and yet in the same moment the

over-riding instinct for self-preservation at all cost,
that was his most outstanding characteristic made
him hurl the girl from him and start for the safety o
the door.

Pentecost fired once, the bullet drilling a nea
hole in the thick glass plate of the tank and formal
dehyde jetting out in a bright stream.

Youngblood straightened slowly and Pentecos
said, "That's better. Hands on head." He gave the
girl a quick push forward. "Now start walking
both of you. I'd like to say do as you're told and you
won't get hurt, but my old granny always taugh
me to tell the truth."

Youngblood moved along the corridor, the girl a
his side, her face white. There was no sign o
Drummond, but that was only to be expected, h
told himself bitterly. The sound of that shot wa
enough to make anyone run for cover.

They went down the stairs under Pentecost'
direction and through a large iron barred door a
the back of the hall. When Pentecost switched o
the light, Youngblood found himself standing on
landing at the top of a flight of steps dropping dow
into what obviously had been a wine cellar at on
time. Now it was painted neatly in white and black
There was a complicated switchboard on one wal
and several steel oven doors in another. Young
blood didn't need anyone to draw a picture for him
This was undoubtedly the crematorium and i
spite of the oppressive warmth, he was suddenl
cold as he went down the steps.

"That will do nicely," Pentecost said and h
moved round to face them, a slight smile on hi
face. "You know where you are?"

"I don't need any blueprint," Youngblood said.

Pentecost reached for a switch on the wall. There was a sudden roar and when he swung back one of the oven doors, they could see flames shooting from all sides of the brickwork through a heavy, armoured glass door.

"Ten minutes," he said. "That's all it takes and afterwards, a handful of ashes."

The girl gave a sudden desperate sob and half collapsed against Youngblood so that he had to catch her. Pentecost circled them warily and stood with his back to the stairs.

"This is what I call the full treatment," he said. "For most people it's a privilege that costs two hundred guineas. You're getting it for free."

Behind him Chavasse vaulted the rail, landing with a soft thud. Pentecost started to turn, but he was too late. Chavasse moved in fast, sliding an arm around the man's neck and wrenched the revolver from his grasp.

He staggered forward, gasping for breath as Chavasse released him with a shove and Youngblood swung him round, his face white with rage and fear.

"You bastard!" he said. "You dirty bastard!" He grabbed Pentecost by the shirtfront and hit him again and again in the face with his right, solid, heavy punches that drove him to his knees.

Chavasse forced his way in between them, pushing Youngblood back against the wall. "All right— that's enough. We want to talk to him!"

"You took your own sweet time getting here, didn't you?" Youngblood said furiously.

Chavasse ignored him. He heaved Pentecost to

his feet and shoved him into a chair that stood beside a small deal table. Pentecost seemed completely dazed and wiped blood from his mouth mechanically with the back of one hand.

"My name's Drummond and this is Harry Youngblood," Chavasse said. "Perhaps you've heard of us?"

Pentecost nodded. "You're the two who escaped from Manningham hospital yesterday. I read about it in the paper."

"Were you expecting us?"

Pentecost hesitated and Youngblood took a step forward, right fist clenched. "Let me speak to him."

Pentecost shrank back defensively, one arm raised. "There's no need for that. I'll tell you anything you want to know."

Chavasse nodded to Youngblood. "All right, give him a chance." He repeated the question. "Were you expecting us?"

Pentecost shook his head. "I had a phone call this afternoon so I was expecting somebody. I didn't know it was going to be you two."

"Who gave you the order?"

"He calls himself Smith. That's all I know about him."

"Can you describe him?"

"Good looking, well spoken." He shrugged. "You'd think he was upper-crust until he starts to work."

Youngblood frowned across at Chavasse. "Mackenzie?"

"It certainly sounds like it." Chavasse looked down at Pentecost again. "Are you expecting him?"

"He didn't say anything definite."

Youngblood had walked across to inspect the ovens and now he turned. "Do you treat everyone Smith sends you like this?"

Pentecost shook his head. "I pass most of them straight through."

Youngblood stared at him in genuine horror. *"Most of them?"* He turned to Chavasse. "For Christ's sake, find out what we have to know and let's get out of here. This bloke gives me the creeps."

"The people you passed on," Chavasse said. "What was their destination?"

Pentecost didn't even hesitate. "I used to leave them at a crossroads five miles from here. They were usually picked up by the same van."

"You stayed to watch?"

Pentecost nodded. "I wasn't supposed to know the destination, but I took the registration number and got a friend of mine with the right contacts to check it for me. The van belongs to a bloke called Bragg. He runs a small boatyard at a little place on the Dorset coast near Lulworth called Upton Magna. It's about ninety miles from here."

Youngblood turned to Chavasse excitedly. "That sounds promising, Drum. It could be the end of the line."

Chavasse nodded slowly, never taking his eyes off Pentecost's face. Quite suddenly he rammed the barrel of the revolver against the man's head and thumbed back the hammer.

"You bloody liar!"

Pentecost panicked completely, his face turning

grey. "It's the truth, I swear it! On my mother's grave I swear it!"

"You never had a mother," Youngblood said in disgust and he hooked away the chair with a foot so that Pentecost fell to the floor.

He lay there shaking with fear and Chavasse looked down at him coldly. There was an account to be settled here, but that would have to wait until a more appropriate time.

He slipped the revolver into his pocket and took Molly's arm. "Come on, let's get out of here."

"What about this?" Youngblood asked, stirring Pentecost with a foot.

"There's nothing he can do," Chavasse said. "If he tries to warn them we're on our way, they'll want to know how we found out where to head for in the first place. How long do you think he'd last after that?"

Pentecost looked at him over his shoulder, eyes widening as the significance of what Chavasse had said sank home and Youngblood laughed harshly.

"You've got a point there. No reason he shouldn't take a rest for a little while though," and he kicked Pentecost in the side of the head.

Pentecost rolled over, struggling for breath, aware of the clang of the door closing at the top of the steps and then he plunged into darkness.

Pain exploding in a chain reaction brought him back from darkness as someone slapped him across the face and a voice repeated his name over and over again. He opened his eyes and stared up into Simon Vaughan's pale face.

"You do look a mess, old man. Presumably they've been and gone?"

Pentecost pushed himself up on one elbow. "There were three of them," he croaked. "Not two like you said. Two men and a girl."

"So that's where she got to! Dear me, I have been careless. Unfortunately I had a little mechanical trouble with the car on the other side of Worcester. I was delayed for the best part of an hour." He helped Pentecost to his feet and sat him in a chair. "When did they leave?"

Pentecost looked at his watch and found that it was almost seven o'clock. "It can't be more than half an hour."

"I see. You told them where to go, did you? Bragg's Boatyard, Upton Magna?" Pentecost stared at him, uncertain of what to say, so confused by the pain in his head that he was unable to think straight and Vaughan sighed. "You shouldn't have done that, you know."

"I couldn't help it," Pentecost said wearily. "They'd have killed me if I hadn't told them. You could probably still catch them."

"I'm sure I can," Vaughan said. "I have two considerable advantages. A very fast car and the fact that I know exactly where I'm going. They, on the other hand, will have to stick to the backroads and check every signpost and the Dorset countryside can be very confusing at night."

Pentecost stirred uneasily as Vaughan moved round behind him. "You know your trouble, old man? You think you've got brains, but you haven't—just a certain amount of low cunning. I can't say it's been a pleasure."

His clenched right fist rose and descended in a hammer blow that splintered the bone at the base of Penetcost's skull. He gave a strange, choking cry and would have tumbled from the chair if Vaughan hadn't held him upright.

He walked round to the front of the chair quickly, dropped to one knee and then straightened, Pentecost draped across his right shoulder in the fireman's lift.

Vaughan crossed to the oven Pentecost had turned on and switched it off. As the flames died away, he opened the glass door and the seven-foot base plate rolled out smoothly on its castors. He dropped Pentecost on to it, arranging his limbs neatly, pushed the plate with its burden back inside and closed the glass door.

He paused to light a cigarette, then pulled the switch. Pentecost's body seemed to jump out of the darkness as great tongues of flame sprang from the brickword to envelop it. His clothing ignited in a second and then, incredibly, an arm was half raised, flaring like a torch and the body moved.

Vaughan watched with interest for a couple of minutes, then closed the outer steel door, turned the dial up to maximum and went up the stairs quickly.

A mile the other side of Gloucester, he pulled up at a phone box and dialled World Wide Exports in London.

"Hello, sweetie, I'm afraid things didn't go according to plan at all here. Our friends are now on their way to Dorset."

"That's a great pity. What are you going to do about it?"

"I think I'd better handle things personally from now on. I'll see they get the usual transportation, but somehow, I don't think they're going to manage to raise a landfall."

"That sounds promising. I'll pass the message along."

"You do that. I'll follow in another boat to report personally. Should be there for breakfast."

"I'll let him know."

The line went dead and Vaughan moved out, whistling softly, got into the Spitfire and drove rapidly away.

10

Three to Four— Rain Squalls

Upton Magna was a fishing village which in other times had enjoyed a considerable importance, but now its population had dwindled to little more than two hundred and there were few boats in the small harbour.

Bragg's boatyard was out on the point beside an old stone jetty, a collection of dilapidated clapboard buildings, untidy stacks of ageing timber and a line of boats hauled clear of the water that looked as if they never expected to sail again.

It was just after half past nine when Vaughan entered the village and drove along the main street. There was a small, whitewashed public house about half way along with a car park behind. He left the Spitfire there, well out of sight in the shadows, and went the rest of the way on foot.

There was a light at the window on the right of the front door of the house directly underneath the faded board sign that carried the legend *George Bragg—Boat-builder—Yachts for hire*. He went up the steps to the rickety porch and peered in through the window.

The room was half office, half living quarters and hopelessly cluttered and untidy. Beyond the wooden reception desk beside the entrance, George Bragg was reading a newspaper at a table which seemed to be covered with a week's accumulation of dirty dishes.

He was well into his sixties, a great bear of a man with a grizzled untidy beard. He got to his feet and, to Vaughan's surprise, reached for a crutch. He picked up an enamel mug and hobbled to the coffee pot on the stove, his right foot dragging awkwardly in a plaster cast.

Vaughan pushed open the door and went inside. Bragg turned quickly in surprise, still holding the mug in one hand and the coffee pot in the other.

"I wasn't expecting you, Mr. Smith."

"What happened to the foot?" Vaughan said.

Bragg shrugged. "Bloody silly, really. Tripped and fell over a pile of scrap on my way through the yard the other night."

"Tanked up to the eyeballs as usual no doubt," Vaughan said. "How bad is it?"

"I've broken a couple of bones."

"Good! As it happens that suits me very nicely. Is the *Pride of Man* ready for sea?"

"As always, just like you ordered. Are you taking her out?"

He was a man stamped with failure. It showed clearly in the broken veins on his face, the bleary drink-sodden eyes, but he was desperately eager to please this strange, dark young man with the white face who was the one thing which had stood between him and ruin for almost two years.

"Not this time," Vaughan said. "But some people will be arriving within the next hour at the outside. Two men and a girl. They'll give you the usual password and they'll expect to be passed on."

Bragg looked dubious. "I'd like to oblige, but I'm not too sure I could make the trip with this foot of mine."

"As I said before, that suits me fine. The foot gives you an excuse not to go. Make it seem even worse than it is. One of the men is a small boat expert anyway—an ex-petty officer in MTBs. He could probably sail the *Pride of Man* round the world if he had to."

"You mean you actually *want* these people to go out on their own?"

"That's right. They'll ask you for a route and destination and you'll give it to them." He smiled. "They won't get there, of course, but there's no reason why they shouldn't travel hopefully for a while."

"What about you?"

"As far as you're concerned I don't exist. I'm going down to the boat now to arrange things. I'll come back along the shore, just in case they turn up early." He produced his wallet, took out five ten pound notes and dropped them on the table. "Fifty now and fifty after they've gone—okay?"

Bragg scooped up the money and stuffed it into his hip pocket. "Fine by me, Mr. Smith. I'll handle it just the way you said."

"See that you do," Vaughan said and the door closed behind him.

Bragg hobbled across to a cupboard by the sink, opened it and took out a bottle of whiskey. There was little more than an inch left in the bottle when he held it up to the light and he cursed softly. He swallowed what there was, tossed the bottle into a corner and sat down at the table to wait for what was to come.

Vaughan went down the stone steps and jumped for the desk of the *Pride of Man*, wet with rain in the sickly yellow light of the single lamp at the end of the jetty. There was no time to waste and he went straight below, peeling off his raincoat as he descended the companionway.

He opened a locker beneath one of the padded bench seats and took out an aqualung and several other pieces of skin-diving equipment which he laid on the centre table.

He knelt down and reached inside the now empty locker. There was a sudden click and the base of the cupboard lifted right out to disclose a secret compartment. There were several interesting items inside. A Sterling sub-machine gun, two automatic rifles, several grenades and half a dozen limpet mines in a straw filled box, each about the size of a dinner plate.

They were harmless until activated, but it was only the work of a minute or so to prime the fuse on one of them. He checked his watch, saw that it was just coming up to ten o'clock and turned the time switch through four complete revolutions. He stripped to his underpants quickly, pulled on the aqualung and went on deck.

He lowered himself over the side, clutching the

mine to his chest with one hand, paused to adjust the flow of air from his aqualung and sank beneath the surface.

The water was bitterly cold, but there was no time to worry about that and he worked his way along to the stern of the boat. At that depth there was enough diffused light from the lamp on the jetty to enable him to see what he was doing and he chose a spot close to the propeller, the limpet mine's powerful electromagnets fastening instantly to the steel hull. He smiled through the visor of his mask and surfaced, well satisfied.

As he crossed the deck to the companionway, a van turned into the yard and halted by the house. As he watched, the lights and engine were switched off and he went down to the saloon quickly.

He replaced the skin-diving equipment in the locker, dressed hurriedly and went back on deck, pulling on his raincoat. As he paused in the shadows, he heard low voices at the end of the jetty as someone approached and went along the lower board-walk quickly, jumped down to the beach and hurried into the darkness.

It was quiet and still when Chavasse cut the Ford's engine and they sat there in the darkness of the boatyard, rain drumming on the roof of the van.

"Well, this is it. The end of the line with any kind of luck."

"It looks like the last place God made," Young-blood said and then the front door opened suddenly beside the lighted window and Bragg appeared, leaning on his crutch.

"Who's out there?"

Chavasse and Youngblood moved forward, Molly a pace or two behind and they halted in a little group at the bottom of the step.

"We're trying to get to Babylon," Chavasse said. "We heard you might be able to help."

Bragg stared at them for a long moment, a frown on his face and then he nodded slowly. "You'd better come in."

He made hard weather of his passage across to the table and sank into his chair with an audible sigh of relief. He wiped sweat from his face with a soiled handkerchief and looked them over curiously.

"I wasn't expecting anyone. They usually give a week's notice."

"We're something special," Chavasse said. "There wasn't time to let you know."

"Well, I'm not sure." Bragg sounded dubious. "The boat's ready to go—always is, but I broke two bones in my foot the other day. Takes me all my time to get to the door and back, never mind make the run to Longue Pierre."

"Longue Pierre?" Chavasse said. "And where would that be?"

"About twelve miles south-west of Alderney in the Channel Islands," Youngblood broke in and grinned as Chavasse turned to him in surprise. "You're forgetting, boy. The Channel was my stamping ground during the war and after it. I know it like the back of my hand."

"He's right," Bragg said. "It ain't much of a place. About a mile across with cliffs three or four hundred feet high on one side. There's only one possible anchorage. That's on the south side of the island. There's an old jetty and not much else."

"Who lives there?"

"Don't ask me, mister. I do what I'm paid to do which is run people across, leave 'em on the jetty and come right back again. There's a house. I know that 'cos I've seen it from the sea, but not much else."

"Who pays you?"

"A fella called Smith. Drops in maybe once in every two or three months, but usually, he just gives me a ring on the phone." He shook his head and looked worried. "Funny I haven't heard from him about you people."

"You will," Youngblood said. "And you'll get paid, I promise you. What kind of boat is it?"

"A motor cruiser—the *Pride of Man*. Thirty footer built by Akerboon. Twin screw, steel hull."

Youngblood whistled. "That's some boat. How is she powered?"

"Penta petrol engine. She'll do about twenty-two knots at full stretch, but not tonight. The weather's not too good."

"What's the report?"

"Wind force three to four with rain squalls and fog in the morning."

"A cake-walk."

"Think you can handle her?" Chavasse asked.

"Handle her? I could sail her across the Atlantic if I had to."

"You'd have a job, mister," Bragg put in. "Her range is only six hundred including the reserve tank."

Youngblood grinned. "Enough and to spare for

passage to the islands. Your troubles are over. You can stay home and watch your foot."

"I don't know," Bragg shook his head. "It's Mr. Smith's boat, not mine."

Youngblood sized him up quickly, taking in the stale whiskey breath, the watery eyes. He pulled out Crowther's wallet, selected a five pound note and dropped it on the table.

"I noticed a nice little pub up the street as we came in. I bet you could drag that leg of yours up there if you really tried."

Bragg looked down at the note hesitatingly, then sighed and stuffed it into his pocket. "I only hope I'm doing the right thing." He opened a drawer and produced a copy of the *Channel Pilot*. "You'd better have this. Three lights on your way out. Keep 'em in line and you can't go wrong."

Youngblood picked up the book and turned to Chavasse, his face alive with a new kind of light. "What are we waiting for?"

The door banged behind them, rattling the frame and Bragg sat there staring into space, a frown on his face. After a while he sighed, put a hand in his pocket and pulled out a handful of money. He looked at it blankly for a moment, then got to his feet and reached for his crutch. A drink, that's what he needed—perhaps two. Something to make him forget the people he had just met, something to shut out the thought of what was going to happen to them out there in the rain and darkness. Most of all, something to make him forget Smith.

He hobbled to the door, took down an oilskin and left.

The *Pride of Man* waited at the end of the jetty and Youngblood took in her flared, raking bow and long sloping deckhouse with a conscious pleasure He was as excited as a schoolboy with a new toy.

"My God, I can't wait to get my hands on her."

Chavasse shook his head. "It's too damned easy."

"What is?" Youngblood demanded impatiently.

"The way Bragg took everything we said. It doesn't make sense. I think I'll go back and see what he's up to."

"Suit yourself," Youngblood said. "But I'm making ready for sea. Anything over ten minutes and you've had it."

He meant every word, so much was obvious, but Chavasse didn't waste time in arguing. He turned back and ran back along the jetty into the darkness of the boatyard.

There had certainly been something indefinable in Bragg's manner which had made him feel uneasy, that was true enough. For one thing the old man's story had been too pat and he carried about him an aura of unctuous villainy, impossible to eradicate.

But more important than that was the fact that he had to get in touch with the Bureau if he was to stand any hope of survival at all once he reached the island and this was his last chance.

He passed the house silently, moved out of the entrance to the yard and paused in the shadows Bragg was swinging along the pavement in front of him looking considerably more agile than he had earlier, in spite of his crutch. He crossed to the little pub and went in and Chavasse moved along the street to the telephone box on the corner.

He dialled his number quickly and was answered almost at once. There was a brief moment when Jean spoke to him and then Graham Mallory was on the line.

"Paul? Where are you?"

"Upton Magna—a little fishing port near Lulworth. Now get this—we're about to leave by boat for an island called Longue Pierre which is twelve miles south-west of Alderney in the Channel Islands. I want to know anything you can tell me about the place and I can only spare you three minutes."

"We're already hooked into Information," Mallory said. "Keep on talking while they're checking."

"You'll want to pull in a lump of dirt called Sam Crowther who runs a place called Wykehead Farm near Settle in Yorkshire. God knows how many he's seen off. Then there's a woman called Rosa Hartman. She lives at Bampton outside Shrewsbury. I'm sorry for her, but she shouldn't have joined."

"Anyone else?"

"A man called Pentecost who has a place called Long Barrow House of Rest outside Gloucester and the old villain I've just been dealing with. Name of Bragg. Runs a boatyard here."

Mallory cut in on him. "Your information on Longue Pierre is coming through now. The island and the only house on it are owned by the States of Guernsey. They've been leased for the past two years to Count Anton Stavru."

"Haven't I heard of him?"

"Very probably. Shady financier always floating big deals that come to grief. Investigated by Fraud

Squad a few times, but he's always managed to get out from under. He's managing director of a firm called World Wide Export. Is any of this helpful?"

"I'll not know till I get there. I'll want some help standing by. Preferably something that can get in fast like a couple of Naval MTBs."

"I'll get on to Naval Intelligence straight away," Mallory said. "If you want to reach them by radio use our usual frequency. Your call sign will be Strongarm. Best of luck."

"I'll need it."

Chavasse dropped the receiver into place, left the box and hurried back along the street to the boatyard. He paused suddenly, dropping into the shelter of an old upturned boat as the door opened and Vaughan stepped out into the porch. He closed the door behind him, cutting off the light and came down the steps.

Chavasse recognised him at once and took Pentecost's revolver from his pocket and waited. Vaughan moved past him and paused, a match flaring in his cupped hands as he lit a cigarette.

Chavasse stood up behind him. "Surprise! Surprise!" he said and drove the butt of the revolver into the back of Vaughan's skull.

He caught him before he could fall, twisting around, bending so that Vaughan fell across his right shoulder. As the engine of the *Pride of Man* shattered the night, he half ran through the darkness toward the jetty.

As he went down the steps, Youngblood was casting off at the stern and he came forward to help Chavasse across the rail wth his burden.

"Well, I'll be damned," he said, looking down

into Vaughan's unconscious face as he sprawled on the deck. "Our old friend Dr. Mackenzie."

"Or Smith or whatever his name is," Chavasse said. "He was just coming out of Bragg's place. I thought it might be nice to ask him along for the ride."

"Stick him in one of the cabins for now," Youngblood advised. "We can have words later. I won't be happy till we're out of here. Molly can give you a hand."

Chavasse went down the companionway holding Vaughan under the armpits and Molly took his feet. They put him on a bunk in one of the three cabins and Chavasse found a length of cord and tied his wrists and ankles securely.

When he turned from locking the door, the girl looked pale and wan as if suddenly, everything was too much for her and he put a hand on her shoulder.

"There should be a galley along here somewhere. Why don't you make us some coffee?"

She brightened a little as if this was something she could at least understand and moved along the passageway. Chavasse watched her go, a frown on his face. A lot had happened and so fast that he'd had little time to speculate about the outcome of things. But what about the girl for whom the events of the past couple of days must have seemed like some dark nightmare? What on earth was going to happen to her? However things turned out she was in for a whole lot of heartbreak.

The poor ugly little bitch. He turned with a sigh and went up the companionway as the *Pride of Man* drifted away from the side of the jetty.

The wind had increased, scattering the rain in

silver clouds through the navigation lights and when he went into the wheelhouse, Harry Youngblood turned and grinned at him, his head disembodied in the light of the binnacle.

"Here we go," he said with a grin and boosted power suddenly, taking the *Pride of Man* round in a long sweeping curve and out through the harbour mouth.

The masthead started to buck as they met the swell and spray scattered across the windows. A couple of points to starboard, the red and green navigation lights of a steamer were visible and Youngblood reduced speed to ten knots and they pushed on into the dark.

"Everything all right?" Chavasse said.

"Bloody marvellous!" There was sheer delight in Youngblood's voice. "This is the life, eh? With any kind of luck we should have a clear run."

It was just coming up to midnight when Chavasse went below to check on Vaughan. When he opened the door and switched on the light, he was at once conscious of the dark eyes staring at him fixedly.

"How do you feel?" he asked.

"How do you expect me to feel?" Vaughan said in a surprisingly strong voice. "The back of my skull crushed in or something very close to it and blood all over my best shirt."

"You're breaking my heart." Chavasse pulled Vaughan into a sitting position and took the mug of coffee that Molly handed to him. "Drink this."

Vaughan swallowed, then gasped. "It'll never replace tea. From the motion, I presume we're on our way across the Channel?"

"That's right."

"What time is it?"

"Round about midnight—why?"

Vaughan started to laugh weakly. "Which means we've passed the point of no return."

Chavasse frowned. "What in the hell are you talking about?"

"It's really rather ironic," Vaughan said. "You see I knew you were on your way to Upton Magna because I had words with friend Pentecost after you'd left."

"And you beat us to it? Bragg was putting on an act, wasn't he?"

"I'm afraid so. I stuck a limpet mine to the hull just before ten o'clock, timed to blow you all to hell in exactly four hours."

"You included."

"To be perfectly honest, that wasn't in the plan at all."

Chavasse untied his ankles and pulled him off the bunk. "Up on the deck and be quick about it."

The *Pride of Man* was lifting well over the heavy swell that scattered spray in a great cascading sheet as they moved along the deck to the wheelhouse. Youngblood turned in surprise as Chavasse pushed Vaughan in ahead of him.

"What's all this?"

Chavasse told him and when he had finished, Youngblood laughed uncertainly. "He's trying to pull a fast one—he must be."

"Suit yourself," Vaughan said.

Chavasse shook his head. "He means it, Harry."

Youngblood stared at him for a long moment and

then throttled down the engine until the boat was making no more than three or four knots and switched to automatic pilot.

"All right, so what are we going to do about it?"

Chavasse turned to Vaughan. "If it's fixed to the hull then you must have used an aqualung and skin-diving gear to put it there. Where is it?"

Vaughan shrugged. "Why not? You'll find it without any trouble anyway. In a locker under one of the bench seats in the saloon."

"There's your answer, Drum," Youngblood said. "As long as we can reach it, it can be defused."

"Sorry to disappoint you and all that, but not this baby," Vaughan said. "It can only be defused after complete dismantling and you have neither the equipment nor the facilities."

"Electromagnetic, I suppose?" Chavasse said.

Vaughan nodded. "And this tub has a steel hull so you'll never prise it loose, not under the conditions you're faced with. Try too hard and the damned thing might blow up anyway."

"What type is it?"

"Getting technical are we? But of course, I was forgetting—you were a captain in the Royal Engineers, weren't you?"

"Never mind the funny stuff," Youngblood said savagely. "Just answer him."

"Martinet Mark 4, and much good may it do you."

Chavasse burst into sudden laughter, unable to contain the wave of elation that swept through him and the smile died on Vaughan's face.

"What's so damned funny?"

"You are," Chavasse said. "You're a hundred

thousand laughs." He turned to Youngblood. "If you'll stop the engines for about ten minutes, Harry, I'll find the aqualung he mentioned and go over the side."

"You mean you can fix it?" Youngblood said incredulously.

"To all intents and purposes, but I'll explain later. Just look after baby for me, will you?" And Chavasse moved back along the deck and went below.

It was bitterly cold down there in the dark water as he felt his way along the hull until he located the mine. He found the time switch and hung there for a moment, testing it with his fingers. If Vaughan had timed the explosion to take place within four hours then he must have moved the switch through four complete revolutions and the maximum was twelve. Chavasse turned the switch, counting slowly. Only when it refused to turn any more did he release his hold and drift up to the surface.

Youngblood and Molly helped him over the rail and he swore softly as the girl hauled on his left arm and pain coursed through him like fire.

"You all right, Drum?" Youngblood said anxiously.

"I am now." Chavasse turned to Vaughan who stood by the companionway, wrists tied in front of him. "Simple when you know how. The Martinet is a short term time bomb extensively used by both the Army and Navy. The timing device operates up to a maximum of twelve hours. All I had to do was move it on from the time of your choice. Right round the clock till we reached neutral again."

"You mean you've defused it?" Youngblood demanded.

"To all intents and purposes."

Vaughan sighed and shook his head. "We learn something new every day. What time do we reach Longue Pierre?"

"Seven-thirty or thereabouts," Youngblood said. "Why?"

"It's just that I can't wait to get there, old man," Vaughan said. "I'm sure it's going to be a barrel of laughs for everyone." He turned and disappeared down the companionway whistling cheerfully.

11

Fog in the Morning

Chavasse came awake to find Molly leaning over him, her hand on his shoulder. He had gone to sleep on one of the bench seats in the saloon and he swung his legs to the floor and took the mug of coffee she offered.

He swallowed some gratefully. "That's better. What time is it?"

"Six a.m."

"My God, have I slept that long?"

He went up the companionway, his coffee in one hand. Water slopped over the starboard rail and cold rain lashed his face as he walked along the heaving deck and went into the wheelhouse.

Youngblood turned to look at him briefly. "How do you feel?"

"My arm hurts like hell, but I can use it, which is something. What about you?"

"I'm enjoying myself. There's been quite a sea running for an hour or more now. Likely to get worse before it gets better."

"Will it affect our time of arrival?"

"If you'd like to take the wheel I'll have another look at the chart."

Chavasse squeezed past, slipping into the pilot's seat and Youngblood went to the chart table. He made one or two calculations and threw down his pencil, stretching his arms.

"We could be a little earlier than I thought. It all depends on the way the weather goes. Think you can handle her for a while?"

"I don't see why not."

"I'll take a break—maybe Molly can find me something to eat. Afterwards, we'd better talk things over. We still don't know what we're getting into. Maybe it's about time we put the squeeze on our friend."

Chavasse nodded. "We'll see."

The door banged and he leaned back in the seat, one hand on the wheel and lit a cigarette. Already the darkness was fading, a faint pearly luminosity touching the water and he strained his eyes into the grey waste of morning, wondering what lay ahead.

One thing was certain. Whatever other difficulties might present themselves, in the final analysis, his greatest problem was still going to be Harry Youngblood himself and what to do with him.

He remembered their first meeting in the cell at Fridaythorpe and how it had confirmed the impression he had already gained from a close study of the man's file at Bureau headquarters. That in spite of the newspaper stories and romanticised magazine features, Youngblood beneath it all, was a brutal and resourceful criminal who would smash down anything or anybody that got in his way and who would stop at nothing to get what he wanted.

Having said that, the fact remained that for many weeks they had been comrades of a sort in that strange sub-world that is life in any large prison. On the other hand, if Chavasse had not gained possession of Smith's gun the night of the break from the hospital and forced the issue, Youngblood would never have taken him along, in spite of the fact that Chavasse had saved him from death, or at least serious injury, on two occasions in the machine shop.

And then there was Molly. If she'd turned her back at the farm, things would have taken their usual course and their journey might have ended at the bottom of Crowther's well and yet Youngblood had been prepared to ditch her without a qualm until it had become obvious that she might still be useful.

Even at the end and in spite of the fact that Chavasse had pulled him out of trouble again at Long Barrow, Youngblood had been prepared to leave in the boat without him. He was without a single redeeming feature, a selfish egomaniac who had never in his life thought of anyone besides himself. Plenty of men had spent their early years in an orphanage, others had known a hard war—how many had taken Harry Youngblood's road?

Chavasse sighed heavily and dropped his cigarette to the floor. All true, every word of it, which didn't make it any easier to send him back to gaol for another fifteen years—possibly even more now.

He looked back on his own four months inside, remembering the filth, the squalor, the grey faces, the long empty days and was suddenly almost physically sick so that he opened a window quickly and drew in great lungfuls of damp salt air.

The door swung open behind him and Youngblood came in grinning hugely, rain on his face. "I haven't felt like this for years. My God, Drum, I realise what I'd been missing."

He took over the wheel and Chavasse leaned against the door watching him. He knew his stuff, there was no question of that and he increased speed, racing the dirty weather that threatened in the east.

The *Pride of Man* soared over the waves like a living thing, water cascading across the prow in a green curtain and Youngblood laughed aloud in a kind of ecstasy.

Chavasse found it impossible not to respond. "A hell of a change from that cell in Fridaythorpe."

"Fridaythorpe?" For a brief moment Youngblood's smile was wiped clean. "I'll tell you something, Drum," he said, his face all iron. "I'd send this tub to the bottom and go with her before they'd get me back there."

He increased power, the *Pride of Man* lifting out of the water and Chavasse, feeling unaccountably sad, turned and went out on deck.

He had a bacon sandwich and more coffee with Molly and then went to check on Vaughan. He was lying on his bunk face to the wall and when he turned, looked paler than ever.

"What's wrong with you?" Chavasse demanded, hauling him into a sitting position.

"Some people have the stomach for this kind of

life, old man—others haven't. They said Nelson was sick every time he put to sea or didn't you know?"

Chavasse pulled him off the bunk, pushed him along the passage way to the saloon and shoved him down into a chair.

"How about some coffee?"

"Now that I wouldn't mind."

Chavasse nodded and Molly filled one of the enamel mugs and pushed it across the table. Vaughan lifted it in both hands, his wrists still tied.

"I don't know how long it will stay down," he said. "But we can but try."

Chavasse lit a cigarette and put it between Vaughan's lips. "And now we talk."

"Do we, old man? That's nice."

"It won't be if you persist in being awkward. Who are we going to find on Longue Pierre—the Baron?"

"God help you if you do."

"What kind of a set-up does he have there?"

Vaughan smiled pleasantly. "Now you really can't expect me to answer that. A breach of faith."

Chavasse sighed. "You know you're putting me in a very awkward position. I may even have to send Youngblood down to talk to you and I wouldn't like that."

"He doesn't worry me in the slightest."

"He should do. I think you're forgetting an important item. I'm just an amateur compared to Youngblood. He knows that if they get their hands on him he goes back inside for fifteen years and they'll watch him every minute of the time. He'll never get out again."

"So what?"

"He'd cut your throat if he thought it was necessary to prevent that happening."

Vaughan showed not the slightest sign of fear, but he stopped smiling and frowned slightly. He was, in fact, remembering Rosa Hartman's prediction and he smiled again, nodding to himself. No, he would not make it easy for her. If death was to come, then it must find him—he would not go looking for it.

"All right," he said calmly. "The Baron may be on the island or he may not—I honestly don't know. He doesn't come in by boat usually. He has a private helicopter."

"Owned by World Wide Exports of London?"

Vaughan's eyes widened in amazement, then narrowed. "I say, you do know a lot, don't you? Now that *is* interesting. I'll be perfectly honest, old man, and say that I never was very happy about you from the start."

"How big a staff does Stavru keep up at the house?"

Vaughan shrugged. "It depends. Most of the time, there's just a caretaker—a trusted old retainer called Gledik. The Baron—or should I say the Count—is very feudal, you know. Always going on about happy days in dear old Hungary. Loathes the commies."

"But isn't above doing business with them when he has some expensive merchandise to sell?"

"Just like Alice—curiouser and curiouser." Vaughan's eyes flared with a strange green light. "I've a nasty feeling we've all been had where you're concerned, old man."

"Isn't that a shame?"

Chavasse killed the conversation stone dead at that point by hauling Vaughan to his feet, running him back along the passageway and locking him in his cabin. When he returned to the saloon, Molly was still sitting at the table. It was obvious that the conversation had been completely meaningless to her and he paused and tilted her chin.

Her eyes had dropped back into their sockets and were red and angry from lack of sleep. Her skin was blotched and unsightly and she seemed completely exhausted.

"I don't like him, Paul," she said. "He frightens me."

"He can't harm you—not now." Chavasse patted her shoulder. "Why not lie down for a while? You look all in."

She nodded wearily and followed him obediently like a small child when he took her into one of the cabins. She lay on a bunk and he covered her with a blanket and left.

When he went up to deck, it was still raining hard, but the sea was a lot calmer. Youngblood's face was lined with fatigue in the grey light of morning, but his smile was as indefatigable as ever.

"We've just raised Alderney," he said and pointed to a grey-green smudge on the horizon.

"How long?"

"Half an hour. I'm giving her full power now things are calmer. The only thing we have to worry about is the fog."

"Is it likely to be bad?"

"Can't say, but it's coming in fast. On the other hand it does give us some kind of cover for the approach."

"I've just been having words with our friend below."

"Get anything out of him?"

"Apparently the Baron comes in and out by helicopter."

"Is he there now?"

"Says he doesn't know."

Youngblood shook his head. "I can't believe that. Maybe we'd better try a little persuasion."

"You'd be wasting your time. I get a distinct impression that he's the type which doesn't crack easily and I think he was telling the truth. Most of the time there's just a caretaker in residence up at the house."

"Then what do we do?" Youngblood said. "I've had a good look at the chart and Bragg was right. The jetty is the only possible anchorage. If we go in there, we could run slap into trouble."

"I've been thinking about that and I've had an idea of sorts. Let's have another look at the chart."

Youngblood switched to automatic pilot and joined him. "You're wasting your time if you're hoping to find somewhere else we can land. I've been over that chart a dozen times."

Chavasse nodded. "I had something different in mind. The house is in a hollow on the western slope. If we approached from the east where the highest cliffs are, we wouldn't be seen, especially in the fog."

Youngblood shook his head. "There isn't any possible anchorage on that side."

"Maybe not, but it looks to me as if there are plenty of places where a small boat could land."

Youngblood looked dubious. "It sounds all right

in theory, but I know these waters. It's more than probable that a small boat couldn't survive in the kind of surf you'll find at the bottom of those cliffs."

"It could well be that we just don't have any choice." Chavasse shrugged. "We'll just have to wait and see."

They crept in towards the island through a grey shroud that seemed to go on forever and somewhere the surf boomed angrily like distant thunder.

The *Pride of Man* was making no more than two or three knots, her engine muted and Youngblood stood at the wheel, straining anxiously into the fog, feeling for the cross currents that would tell him he was getting close.

Chavasse was in the prow and suddenly, he pointed dead ahead and called excitedly. In the same moment the wind which had been strengthening noticeably for at least half an hour, tore a great hole in the curtain, giving a breath-taking view of the cliffs dead ahead.

They were perhaps two hundred yards away, the tops completely shrouded in grey, thousands of sea birds nesting on their rocky ledges and beneath them, the surf pounded in across jagged rocks.

Chavasse moved back to the wheelhouse as they went closer. "What do you think?"

Youngblood shook his head. "It doesn't look too good to me."

He approached to within fifty yards of the base of the cliffs and turned as the waves started to pull them in. Chavasse pointed to a horseshoe amongst the rocks and the strip of shingle beyond it.

"That looks something like."

Youngblood shook his head. "I still say the dinghy wouldn't last five minutes in that surf."

"What if I wore the aqualung?"

Youngblood turned quickly. "Now you're talking. I'd give you a better than even chance, always remembering that arm of yours."

"Well, you can't go, that's obvious," Chavasse said. "It looks as if I'm elected."

He went below, opened the locker in the saloon and took out the skin-diving equipment. Whatever else happened it was going to be cold out there—damned cold and he stripped quickly and pulled on the close fitting diving suit in black rubber. He slipped Pentecost's revolver into one of the pockets, zipped it up and went back on deck carrying the aqualung.

Youngblood stopped engines and joined him hurriedly. "Let's make it quick. The current could have us on those rocks before you know it."

"Give me an hour," Chavasse said as they unshipped the dinghy from its davits. "Then come back for a look. If I stay back on the shingle, that means I want you to sail round to the jetty. If I stand in the surf, then the whole think stinks. You'd better let me have your watch."

Youngblood unstrapped it and handed it across. "What will you do then?"

"I'll try to swim back to the boat."

Youngblood laughed harshly. "Rather you than me. Let's have her over then."

The dinghy was constructed of fibreglass and was therefore extremely light. They put her over the stern between them and Youngblood held on to the line while Chavasse struggled into the straps of his aqualung. He pulled the visor down over his face, adjusted the air flow and went over the side. Youngblood waved, the line went slack and as he reached for the oars, the current jerked him away.

The wind was freshening, lifting the waves into whitecaps and as he reached for the oars, the dinghy heeled and water poured in over the gunn'l. He adjusted his weight and started to row.

The engines coughed into life and the *Pride of Man* started to move away, but he had no time to watch its progress. He glanced over his shoulder and through the curtain of spray, the cliffs loomed larger, the surf boiling in over ragged, dangerous looking rocks. There was a hollow drumming on the hull of the dinghy and it spun round several times, grazing a black razor edge that would undoubteldy have split it neatly in half.

It was no good—his left arm simply didn't have the strength to haul on that oar under such extreme conditions. He tried desperately to control the dinghy with just the right hand, but it was no good. The oar was snatched away by a sudden fierce eddy and he grasped the sides and waited.

The cliffs were very close now, the sea breaking over great ledges of rock in a dirty white foam and behind him, a great heaving swell rolled in, sweeping the dinghy before it.

He went over the stern, water closing over his head for only a moment or so. He surfaced in time to see the dinghy smashed down against the first line of rocks. Another wave lifted it high into the air, then it bounced across the reef twice and disintegrated.

There was a great smooth funnel in the rocks to

the right and as another great swell lifted behind him, he dived and started to swim towards it, his webbed feet driving him through the water.

There was turbulence all around him, thousands of white bubbles and a great curtain of sand and grit and then he was lifted up as if by a giant hand. He surfaced, aware of the smooth black sides of the funnel on either side of him and suddenly found himself lying, arms outstretched, sprawled across a great moving bank of sand and shingle.

A giant hand seemed to be trying to pull him back and he crawled forward on hands and knees. Again the sea washed over him in a green curtain and as it receded, he staggered to his feet and stumbled forward. A moment later he was safe on the strip of beach at the foot of the cliffs.

The *Pride of Man*, on automatic pilot, cruised at a steady three knots, four hundred yards out from the cliffs and Youngblood stood at the rail watching Chavasse through a pair of binoculars he had found in the wheelhouse.

The tiny black figure on the beach waved once and then the curtain of mist dropped into place, hiding him from view.

Youngblood lowered the binoculars. "So far, so good," he said softly. "And now we wait."

He turned from the rail and went down the companionway to the saloon. There was no sign of Molly, but when he called her name, she answered from the galley and he found her at the stove making more coffee.

"I thought you were trying to get some sleep," he said.

She shook her head. "I just couldn't—I've got a splitting headache."

"Paul's gone ashore to see how the land lies," he told her. "So we'll be just cruising around for the next hour till we hear from him. Bring me up some coffee when it's ready."

He moved back along the passageway and paused as a thunderous kicking commenced on one of the cabin doors and Vaughan called to him.

"I say, old man, have you got a moment?"

Youngblood unlocked the door. "What do you want?" he said ungraciously.

"Where's Drummond?"

"Gone ashore."

"Has he, indeed? Now that was enterprising of him. On the other hand he seems a very resourceful sort of chap altogether, our Mr. Drummond. I must say I'd love to know how he found out who the Baron is."

Youngblood frowned. "What in the hell are you talking about?"

"Count Anton Stavru—the Baron," Vaughan said. "Drummond seemed to know all about him when we were having words half an hour or so ago."

Youngblood grabbed him by the front of his jacket, pulled him into the passageway and pushed him along to the saloon. He flung him down into a chair and stood over him threateningly.

"Now let's get this clear. You say Drummond told you he knows the Baron was this bloke Stavru?"

"That's right, old man. He even knew about our London front—World Wide Exports. To be perfectly honest, he seemed remarkably well informed to me."

"So it would seem," Youngblood said, his face dark.

Vaughan registered innocent surprise. "Don't tell me he didn't take you into his confidence?"

Youngblood didn't seem to hear him. His face had gone white and a vein bulged in his forehead just above one eye. He turned suddenly, plunged towards the companionway and went up on deck.

Vaughan started to laugh, his bound hands stretched out before him across the table and Molly, who had just come in from the galley, stood staring at him, a mug of coffee in one hand.

"Now I call that very, very funny indeed." He looked at her enquiringly. "Don't you think so?"

She eased past him on the other side of the table, a look of fear on her face and went up the companionway quickly.

Vaughan's smile disappeared and he was on his feet in an instant and moving towards the galley. He went straight to the cutlery drawer next to the sink, opened it and searched for the bread knife. He closed the drawer on the handle so that the blade stood up and set to work on the rope that linked his wrists. He was free within a couple of minutes and hurried back into the saloon.

He dropped to one knee, opened the locker beneath the bench seat and felt for the secret catch. He had made his choice in advance and stood up, the Sterling submachine gun in his hands. He checked the action quickly, then went up the companionway to the deck.

Youngblood was at the rail, binoculars raised as

he searched for Chavasse through the mist and Molly stood at his left side holding his mug of coffee.

"Can you see him?" she said.

Youngblood nodded. "He's still on the beach. Must be looking for a way up."

There was an audible click behind them as Vaughan cocked the Sterling and Youngblood swung around.

"Nice and easy," Vaughan said. "And don't try anything silly and heroic, there's a good chap."

The girl gave a tiny cry of alarm and dropped the mug of coffee on the deck, clutching at Youngblood's sleeve. He pushed her away violently.

"Get off me, you stupid bitch!"

"Now then, old man, don't lose your temper. Just walk along to the wheelhouse and get this tub moving."

"And where are we supposed to be going?" Youngblood said.

"Straight into harbour as fast as we can. I want to be on hand when your friend Drummond turns up at the house, just to see the look on his face when he finds us all waiting for him."

Chavasse shrugged off the aqualung, stripped the great rubber fins from his feet and left them in a crevasse in the rocks which seemed to be well out of reach of the sea.

The cliffs towered above him into the mist, black and green, glistening with rain and spray, certainly completely unclimbable at this point and he started to work his way along the narrow strip of beach, clambering over boulders, in one place wading waist-deep, hanging on to the rocks for dear life as the sea threatened to pull him out again.

He spent at least twenty minutes in this way and at last found a section where several great fissures and gullies presented an easy if strenuous route to the top.

He climbed steadily, pausing for a breather halfway up, turning to look out to sea. The mist seemed to have thickened again and he could see no sign of the *Pride of Man* and he turned and started to climb.

The sound of the sea faded behind him, but in spite of the coldness of the rain and wind, he sweated heavily in the close fitting rubber suit and the pain in his left arm was constant and nagging, refusing to go away, even when he didn't use it. Blood trickled from beneath the rubber cuff of the sleeve in a thin stream, indicating the probability that some of the stitches had burst, but there was nothing he could do about that now.

He scrambled over the edge a moment or two later and lay face down in the wet grass for a while. Finally, he sat up and looked at Youngblood's watch. It was almost half past eight—later than he had imagined and he got to his feet and started up the gentle turf slope.

He reached the top and crouched suddenly. Below him was a large natural crater about fifty feet deep and two hundred across and a helicopter was parked squarely in the centre.

The other side of the crater was fringed by a line of pine trees, but there was no sign of the house which, from what he recalled of the map, was lower down the slope towards the other side of the island.

He went down into the crater and ran toward the

helicopter quickly. It stood there waiting for him, strangely alien in that grey world of mist and rain and he clambered up the side ladder and unscrewed the engine canopy quickly.

There were several things he could have done to put the machine out of action without damaging the engine, but he had no time for such niceties. He selected a large and jagged stone, clambered back up the ladder and proceeded to smash as much as he would within the space of thirty seconds, paying particular attentin to the fuel supply. As the fumes of the high octane petroleum drifted into the damp air, he dropped to the ground and moved across to the shelter of the trees.

The house stood in another hollow a couple of hundred yards down the slope on the other side of the trees, but he was unable to see the inlet from that position. There was a path over to the left and he cut across to join it and started to run down towards the house.

He crouched beside a bush on the edge of the wood, the revolver in his hand and looked across a neglected lawn at the rear of the house towards a stone terrace and french windows. One of them stood slightly ajar, the end of a red velvet curtain billowing out into the rain.

He crossed to the house keeping to the line of a hedge for shelter and moved to the french windows. The curtains were completely drawn so that it was impossible to see inside. He hesitated for only a moment, then pulled the curtain back and stepped in.

The room seemed to be in complete darkness, which was only an illusion of course, but before his eyes had a chance to become accustomed to the change of light, something hard was rammed against the side of his head.

A familiar voice said, "I'll take that, old man," and the revolver was plucked from his grasp.

A light was snapped on in the same moment. There were five other people in the room besides himself. Vaughan, who stood on the right, a Sterling sub-machine gun in his hands and Youngblood and Molly over by the door, guarded by a grey-haired ageing man whose brown face was a patchwork of wrinkles.

The man who got up from the easy chair by the empty fireplace to come forward was one of medium height and wore a thigh-length hunting jacket with a fur collar, a green Tyrolean hat slanted across a surprisingly amiable face. He was obviously somewhere in his sixties and carried himself with the assurance of the natural aristocrat.

"Come in Mr. Drummond or should I say Mr. Chavasse? We've been waiting for you." He laughed lightly. "Welcome to Babylon."

12

Alas Babylon

Youngblood pushed forward, bewilderment on his face. "What is all this?"

"You might well look puzzled, Mr. Youngblood," Stavru said. "Allow me to enlighten you. Your friend Drummond is in reality an agent of the Special Branch at Scotland Yard. His name is Chavasse—Paul Chavasse—and he was apparently put into Fridaythorpe Gaol to keep an eye on you. It would seem your bid for freedom was anticipated."

"A copper?" Youngblood said. "Him?" He laughed incredulously. "Not in a thousand years. I can smell one upwind a mile away. If he's a copper, I'm a monkey's uncle."

"So?" Stavru turned to Chavasse, eyes narrowed. "I value your expert opinion. It would seem Mr. Chavasse may well be an agent of another sort." He nodded to the grey haired man. "Take Mr. Youngblood and the young lady down to the cellar, Gledik, then I want you to go and make the helicopter ready for flight. We leave in thirty minutes."

"Now look here . . ." Youngblood started, but

Gledik simply stepped back and took careful aim with the Luger he was holding.

"You'll have to excuse Gledik," Stavru said. "A session with the AVO in Budapest involved him in the loss of his tongue, but he's extraordinarily efficient. I would do what he says if I were you."

The door closed behind them and he turned with a smile and produced his cigarette case. "Do have one, my dear chap, and let's get down to business. You and I are, how would you put it, professionals? We know the score."

Chavasse accepted the cigarette and a light. "Depends on how you look at it."

"What are you—M.I.5 or 6?" Chavasse didn't reply and Stavru's eyebrows raised fractionally. "Something special eh? A compliment, I must say. I like the fake robbery touch to get you into prison. Highly ingenious."

"Actually it was the real thing," Chavasse said, deciding for the moment to keep things on the same level. "We felt that only the best was good enough. I must say you've got quite an organisation."

"As the advertising types are so fond of saying, we try to give our customers a service."

"Some service. An early grave for the suckers like George Saxton and Ben Hoffa who were mug enough to fall for the glossy brochure and allowed their cash to pass over in advance."

"Strange as it may seem, Mr. Chavasse, there is no one quite as gullible as your professional criminal. Their capacity for swallowing any kind of a tall story, hook, line and sinker, never ceases to amaze me."

"And the ones—the ones you pass on who ended

up East of the Iron Curtain? They must have been gold on the hoof."

"Very much so, I assure you. In fact it occurs to me that certain parties on that side of the political fence might be more than interested in bidding for you, my friend. Every man has his price, in more ways than one."

Chavasse flicked his cigarette out into the rain. "In the circumstances, I'm sure you'll appreciate my understandable curiosity as to how you found out about me?"

Stavru crossed to an oak sideboard and poured himself a brandy from a cut glass decanter. "A very recent discovery, I assure you, but like a good journalist, I never disclose my sources. And now you must excuse me. I have certain preparations to make before we leave." He nodded to Vaughan. "Take him down to the others, Simon, then come back here."

"Youngblood and the girl—what's going to happen to them?" Chavasse said as Vaughan pushed him towards the door.

"They will be well taken care of, I assure you."

Stavru turned, dismissing him completely and Vaughan opened the door. "Don't take it to heart, old man. They won't feel a thing—really they won't. I give you my word."

The cellar into which Vaughan pushed him was in almost total darkness, a patch of light showing from a tiny window on the other side which was far too small to be used as an exit.

As the door closed behind him there was a rustle

on the other side of the room and Youngblood came forward.

"Who's that?"

"It's me—Paul."

There was a moment of stillness during which Chavasse prepared himself for some sudden blow, but it never came and when Youngblood spoke, he sounded strangely subdued.

"Those things he said about you upstairs—they were all true?"

"That's right."

Youngblood turned away, exploding angrily. "Me, Harry Youngblood, taken in by a bloody copper."

Chavasse could have pointed out that without his assistance, Youngblood's journey would have come to an abrupt halt at Wykehead Farm, but he knew that he would be wasting his time.

"If you want to know, I couldn't care less about you and your friends and I'm not a policeman. Stavru happens to run a nice little sideline in the sale of state secrets and traitors to people who aren't on exactly friendly terms with our government. The department I work for has one main interest—to see that he's stopped."

"Which would include making sure that I went back to gaol for fifteen years," Youngblood said. "Or did you intend to let me go free?"

"That kind of decision isn't mine to make."

"My God, after all I've done for you." Youngblood turned away, shaking with rage and Molly moved out of the darkness to clutch at his arm.

"What's going to happen, Harry?"

He turned on her angrily, shoving her violently

from him so that she hit the opposite wall. "Get away from me, you stupid little whore."

She sank on to a bench, crying steadily and Chavasse lit a cigarette. "Does that make you feel any better?"

"Why don't you get stuffed?" Youngblood peered out of the window for a moment and turned suddenly. "What happens now? Did he give you any idea?"

"Do I have to draw you a picture?"

"Maybe I could make a deal?" Youngblood said eagerly.

"With what? He's got your diamonds, hasn't he? What does he want with you? You're supposed to be at the bottom of the well back there at Wykehead."

"But there must be something," Youngblood cried and there was an edge of hysteria in his voice.

Chavasse moved past him, pulled himself up to the window and looked out at ground level across the courtyard. As he watched, Gledik appeared from the trees and ran across to the house quickly.

Chavasse dropped to the ground and turned with a faint smile. "I think we'll see some action soon."

It came within three or four minutes. Footsteps hurried along the passageway, the door was thrown open and light flooded in as Vaughan appeared. He had discarded the machine gun and now held a .38 revolver in his right hand. Strangely enough, he seemed rather amused.

"Count Stavru would like a word with you if you can spare a minute, old man," he said to Chavasse. "And be warned—he's very annoyed."

Chavasse glanced at his watch. It was almost nine and he shrugged. "My time is your time. I've certainly nothing better to do." He turned to Youngblood. "If I'm not back in fifteen minutes send out the dogs."

But Youngblood failed to respond, turning away with an angry exclamation and Chavasse sighed and moved out into the passage ahead of Vaughan.

Stavru was standing by the fireplace talking to Gledik in Hungarian and he turned quickly as Chavasse and Vaughan came in. He was like a different man, the skin drawn tightly over his cheekbones, the eyes cold and hard.

"I understand from Gledik that the engine of the helicopter has been damaged beyond repair. Presumably this was your doing?"

"That's right."

"That was very foolish of you."

"I don't think so." Chavasse walked to the sideboard and calmly poured himself a glass of brandy. "You're not going anywhere, Stavru. You're finished—all washed up. Before we left Upton Magna last night I phoned through to my headquarters in London. I told them about Longue Pierre and they did a quick check and came up with you, so now everyone's happy. By the way, I shouldn't waste your time trying to get hold of World Wide Exports today—I don't think they'll be open for business."

Stavru turned to Vaughan. "You think he is telling the truth?"

"Very probably."

"Which means his friends may come down on us at any time."

"That's right," Chavasse said smoothly. "Courtesy of the Royal Navy."

Stavru shrugged. "The situation is certainly inconvenient, but not impossible. The *Pride of Man* is a very fast boat. We can be in French territorial waters within ten minutes of leaving here."

"You can always try," Chavasse said, inventing freely. "But I think you'll find that the French coastguard and police are prepared in advance for just such a move."

"It would seem you have thought of everything." Stavru walked to the french windows and stood there looking out at the rain. Suddenly he swung around and there was something close to excitement on his face. "But perhaps not?" he said softly and turned to Vaughan. "Get Youngblood up here, Simon, and quickly. There's no time to lose."

"There's no way out, you know," Chavasse said.

"You have a saying, do you not, Mr. Chavasse? Desperate situations breed desperate remedies."

He poured himself another drink and a moment later, Youngblood was pushed into the room. He stood there, hands clenching and unclenching nervously, a wary expression on his face and Stavru moved to meet him.

"Mr. Youngblood, I have just discovered some rather unpleasant news. Mr. Chavasse's wolves could apparently descend on us at any moment."

"That's your hard luck."

"And yours—or do you look forward to your return to your cell at Fridaythorpe for the next fifteen years?"

Youngblood's face was his answer and Stavru laughed gently. "Then we can do business. I understand that at one time you were a Petty Officer on torpedo boats in your Royal Navy and that after the war you were engaged in the running of contraband across the channel."

"So what?"

"You brought the *Pride of Man* over from England by night in not very pleasant weather which would seem to indicate your competence. Could you sail her to Portugal?" He turned to Chavasse. "I should perhaps explain that the boat is registered in Liberia. It would therefore be completely illegal for even the Royal Navy to attempt to board her at sea."

"Her range is only six hundred," Youngblood said. "You'd need enough extra juice for another three or four hundred miles, just to take care of contingencies."

"There is plenty of petrol on the jetty in twenty gallon drums."

"All right—what's in it for me?"

"Your continued freedom and, of course, your diamonds or their equivalent in Swiss francs. As a matter of interest, I would be setting up a new organisation in Tangiers. I think we might do very well together."

"Don't listen to him, Harry," Chavasse said. "You'd never get across the Bay of Biscay in a boat like that. It's the wrong time of year."

"Who says I wouldn't?" Youngblood smiled recklessly. "I'd take that tub to hell rather than go back to Fridaythorpe." He turned to Stavru. "How do I know I can trust you?"

Stavru's hand came out of his pocket clutching a Luger. He held it out, a slight smile on his face. "Would this constitute a satisfactory token?"

Youngblood satisfied himself that the weapon

was loaded and grinned as he pushed it into his hip pocket. "Okay, let's get started. The sooner we get those drums on board, the sooner we get out of here."

Stavru nodded and turned to Vaughan. "Take Mr. Chavasse back to the young lady and come back as quickly as you can. I want you to help me clear up the essentials in the house. Gledik can go down to the jetty with Mr. Youngblood to load the fuel."

"Is it in order to ask what you're going to do with us?" Chavasse said.

Vaughan smiled. "I'm sure I'll think of something, old man."

As he was pushed towards the door, Chavasse turned in appeal to Youngblood. "They're going to kill us, Harry, you know that."

"That's your hard luck."

"What about Molly?"

"She shouldn't have joined. Nobody asked her to."

"And that's your last word?"

Youngblood's face was suddenly suffused with passion. "Well what do you expect me to say, for Christ's sake? You've got to look out for number one in this life."

He turned angrily and went out through the french windows, Gledik at his heels and Stavru came forward. "Sad, isn't it, but that's life, my friend."

"Even sadder is the fact that a man only ever reaps what he sows," Chavasse told him and he turned and went out, Vaughan a couple of paces ahead of him.

*   *   *

As the cellar door closed behind him, Molly got up from the bench and came forward anxiously. "Where's Harry? What have they done to him?"

"He's fine," Chavasse said soothingly. "He's gone down to the jetty."

She stared at him blankly. "I don't understand."

He pushed her gently down on the bench. "They're leaving, Molly, and Harry's going with them. They need him to run the boat."

"But what about me?" she said. "He wouldn't leave me? He'll take me with him?"

"I wouldn't count on that."

She got to her feet, her eyes wild. "They're taking him by force, aren't they?" She turned without waiting for an answer. "What can we do, Paul? There must be something."

There was obviously nothing to be gained from any further discussion and Chavasse didn't try. It was almost half past nine now and he lit a cigarette and sat down on the bench.

Vaughan would be coming very soon and there was nothing he could do about that either. Whatever happened, it would be handled with ice-cold efficiency and with no chances offered for sudden grabs or in-fighting. The man was too much of a professional to make silly mistakes. No point in telling the girl—it would only make it harder for her.

There was a footstep in the passage outside, the rattle of the bolt and the door opened. Vaughan stayed well back, the gun in his right hand as steady as a rock.

"Outside, we're taking a little walk."

"I want to speak to Stavru," Chavasse said. "Tell him I'm ready to make a deal."

"He doesn't need one, old man, and you're too late anyway. He's gone down to the boat. In fact we're just about ready for off."

The girl seemed completely bewildered by all this. "What's happening, Paul? Where are we going?"

"Just do as you're told, sweetie," Vaughan said. "Much better in the long run."

They went up the steps from the basement, Vaughan staying well back and somehow there was a terrible inevitability about everything. When they reached the study, Chavasse paused and said desperately, "How do you know they won't clear off without you?"

"With what I've got stored away up here?" Vaughan tapped his forehead and smiled cheerfully. "Don't be silly and keep moving, there's a good chap. We haven't got much time."

It was raining harder than ever as they went out through the french windows and crossed the lawn. It was very quiet in the wood, the only sound the rain hissing down through the branches, and the girl stumbled along in front, Chavasse behind her, Vaughan bringing up the rear.

There would be no sudden warning, no order to halt and turn round, Chavasse knew that. Just a bullet in the back of the head. There was really nothing to lose, no matter how suicidal the situation was and Stavru's words came back into his mind. *Desperate situations breed desperate remedies.*

Molly pushed a branch out of the way as she ploughed through the wet grass. Chavasse caught it, held it for only a moment and ducked, allowing it to sweep back into Vaughan's face. He staggered back with a cry of alarm and Chavasse gave Molly a violent push to one side that sent her tumbling down the slope and ran.

A bullet chipped bark from a tree to one side of him, two more sliced branches over his head and he zigzagged desperately. He stumbled and fell and another bullet kicked dirt in his face and he rolled to one side, screaming in sudden agony as stitches tore loose in his left arm.

He staggered forward, head down, aware of the sound of rushing water somewhere ahead and burst through a final screen of bushes to find himself on the banks of a small stream of clear water that brawled its way down to the sea over a bed of smooth stones.

Two more shots sounded, flat and sinister on the damp air and his right leg doubled up suddenly as if kicked and he went headfirst into the water.

He turned over, aware of the blood drifting in a brown cloud from the hole in his leg and tried to get up. He was too late. There was a tremendous crashing in the undergrowth and Vaughan emerged on the bank above.

His face was very pale, ice-cold, intent only on the job in hand. He said nothing, simply raised the revolver and took careful aim. The hammer clicked on an empty chamber. Without a word, his eyes never leaving Chavasse for a moment, he slipped the revolver into one pocket and produced the flick knife from the other. As the blade jumped out of his hand, he stepped into the water and waded forward.

Chavasse's right hand fastened over a large round stone in the stream bed and he brought his arm up and round, hurling it into Vaughan's face with all his remaining strength. It caught him high on the right cheek and he cried out sharply and staggered back, the knife flying from his hand.

It fell into the water a yard or two away, plainly visible on a bed of pebbles and Chavasse rolled over and grabbed for it desperately. He got to one knee, turning just in time to meet Vaughan's forward rush, splitting him cleanly on the razor sharp blade.

Vaughan poised on the edge of eternity, a look of blank amazement on his face and then he actually smiled.

"Well I'll be damned. So the old bitch was right after all."

Blood erupted from his mouth in a sudden bright stream and he turned, took a single hesitant step forward and fell on his face in the water.

Chavasse waded forward and crawled up the bank. He paused to examine his leg and found two holes in the rubber diving suit indicating that the bullet had passed clean through.

It wasn't painful until he stood up and tried to walk and then the pain was bad—really bad, flowering inside him like fire, sweat springing to his forehead. There wasn't much bleeding which was one good thing and he staggered forward, clutching at the pine trees for support as he passed, calling Molly's name aloud.

He was almost at the edge of the wood when he found her huddled under a bush, soaked to the skin. She got to her feet and ran to meet him.

"Thank God. Paul, are you all right?"

"Only just."

"Where's Mr. Smith?"

"Face down in a stream a little way back."

The words meant nothing to her and she clutched at his arm excitedly. "We'll have to hurry if we're going to get down to the jetty in time."

He stared at her blankly. "The jetty? What for?"

"They'll be leaving soon and taking Harry with them. We've got to stop them."

Chavasse held her arms lightly and tried to find the words. "He's going because he wants to go, Molly. He's agreed to take Stavru to Portugal in the boat. In return he gets his freedom and his money."

She laughed—for the first time since he'd known her she laughed. "But that doesn't make sense."

"He left us, Molly. He left us behind to be executed. You never at any time had even a remote prospect of a place in his future."

"You're lying," she said in a low desperate voice. "I don't believe a word of it." She struggled to free herself. "Let me go. If you won't help him, I will."

"No one on top of earth can help Harry Youngblood now."

She went completely rigid, caught by the gravity of his words and Chavasse held up his wrist so that she could see the time.

"The limpet mine, Molly. I didn't switch it through to neutral like I said. I left it on maximum timing—twelve hours. It's the only thing that's kept me going for the past hour."

Her head moved slightly from side to side and there was an expression of real horror on her face.

And then she exploded into action. She kicked at his
shins, fingers hooking at his eyes and suddenly his
leg doubled up beneath him. As he fell, she turned
and ran.

He lay there for a moment or so, his senses
swimming and then forced himself to his feet
and staggered after her, dragging his wounded
leg.

The rain still hammered down remorselessly, but
the mist had cleared a little so that when he went
over the edge of the hollow on the other side of the
house, he could see the tiny harbor below, the boat
tied to the jetty, Stavru and Youngblood standing
in the prow watching Gledik lash half a dozen
drums of petrol together.

Molly was half-way down the hill and running as
she had never run in her life before. There was no
chance on earth of catching her, but Chavasse
gritted his teeth and started down the path.

She called Youngblood's name once, high and
clear and the three men turned to look up towards
her and then she was at the bottom of the path and
ran forward, shouting and waving her arms.

As she put foot on the jetty, the *Pride of Man*
blew up with a tremendous bang that echoed
from the cliffs like thunder. A second later the fuel
tanks went up with a rush and great fingers of fire
lashed out in all directions, pieces of the hull
drifting through it all in a crazy kind of slow
motion.

Chavasse ducked as small pieces of debris whistled through the air above his head, rattling against
the stones of the hillside.

Incredibly, he started to run, all pain forgotten,

sliding down the slope in a shower of earth and stones, picking himself up at the bottom and running into the dense pall of black smoke that enveloped the jetty.

"Molly!" he called. "Molly, where are you!"

But there was no reply—only the crackling of the flames and the stench of burning oil and petrol. The *Pride of Man* had vanished completely taking the three men with her, only the incredibly twisted pieces of steel and superstructure bearing witness to the fact that it had ever existed at all.

But Molly was there, lying face down half way along the jetty. There wasn't a mark on her, that was the strange thing, but she was just as dead and he turned her over gently to her back and slumped down beside her.

For her it was over, all doubts resolved, all passion spent, but not for him. There were people who had to be taken care of—Atkinson, the Principal Officer at Fridaythorpe, for one and somewhere in the organisation of the Bureau or of the Special Branch at Scotland Yard, there was a weak link— the person who had leaked his identity to Stavru. He would have to be found and he would have to be dealt with, but not now—not now.

Somewhere in the distance he could hear the sound of engines, probably the MTBs Mallory had promised to lay on coming in fast to see what all the fuss was about, but it didn't seem to matter any more and he looked down at the dead girl who stared past him into eternity, a look of faint surprise on her face.

"Poor ugly little bitch," he said aloud and for no

reason he could ever satisfactorily explain to himself afterwards, took her hand and held it very
tightly as the first torpedo boat swept in towards
the jetty.